P9-CJJ-715

THE BLOB THAT ATE EVERYONE

This belongs to Mr. S

ARE YOU BRAVE ENOUGH TO READ THESE

?

ALL-NEW! ALL-TERRIFYING!

NOW WITH BONUS FEATURES!
LOOK IN THE BACK OF THE BOOK FOR
EXCLUSIVE AUTHOR INTERVIEWS AND MORE.

Night of the Living Dummy

Deep Trouble

Monster Blood

The Haunted Mask

One Day at HorrorLand
(INCLUDES A SECRET GUIDE TO HORRORLAND!)

Goosebumps®

THE BLOB THAT ATE EVERYONE

R. L. STINE

SCHOLASTIC INC.
New York Toronto London Auckland Sydney
Mexico City New Delhi Hong Kong Buenos Aires

If you purchased this book without a cover, you should be aware that this book is stolen property. It was reported as "unsold and destroyed" to the publisher, and neither the author nor the publisher has received any payment for this "stripped book."

No part of this publication may be reproduced, stored in a retrieval system, or transmitted in any form or by any means, electronic, mechanical, photocopying, recording, or otherwise, without written permission of the publisher. For information regarding permission, write to Scholastic Inc., Attention: Permissions Department, 557 Broadway, New York, NY 10012.

ISBN 0-439-79619-9

Copyright © 1997 by Scholastic Inc. All rights reserved.

The *Goosebumps* book series created by Parachute Press, Inc.
Published by Scholastic Inc.
SCHOLASTIC, GOOSEBUMPS,
and associated logos are trademarks and/or registered
trademarks of Scholastic Inc.

12 11 10   11 12 13 14 15 /0

THE BLOB THAT ATE EVERYONE

1

"I used to believe in monsters," Alex said. She pushed her glasses up on her nose. Her nose twitched. With her pink face and round cheeks, she looked like a tall, blonde bunny rabbit.

"When I was little, I thought that a monster lived in my sock drawer," Alex told me. "You won't believe this, Zackie. But I never opened that drawer. I used to wear my sneakers without socks. Sometimes I tried to go barefoot to kindergarten. I was too scared to open that drawer. I knew the sock monster would bite my hand off!"

She laughed. Alex has the strangest laugh. It sounds more like a whistle than a laugh. *"Wheeeeeeh! Wheeeeeh!"*

She shook her head, and her blonde ponytail shook with her. "Now that I'm twelve, I'm a lot smarter," she said. "Now I know that there is no such thing as monsters."

That's what Alex said to me *two seconds* before we were attacked by the monster.

*   *   *

It was spring vacation, and Alex and I were out collecting things. That's what we do when we can't think of anything better.

Sometimes we collect weird-looking weeds. Sometimes we collect bugs. Or odd-shaped leaves.

Once, we collected stones that looked like famous people. That didn't last long. We couldn't find too many.

If you get the idea that Norwood Village is a boring town — you're right!

I mean, it *was* boring until the monster attacked.

Alex Iarocci lives next door to me. And she is my best friend.

Adam Levin, who lives across town, is my best friend too. I think a person should have a *lot* of best friends!

I'm not sure why Alex has a boy's name. I think it's short for Alexandria. But she won't tell me.

She complains about her name all the time. It gives her a lot of trouble.

Last year at school, Alex was assigned to a boys' gym class. And she gets mail addressed to *Mr.* Alex Iarocci.

Sometimes people have trouble with my name too. Zackie Beauchamp. My last name is pronounced BEECH-am. But no one ever knows how to say it.

Why am I going on about names like this?

I think I know why.

You see, when the Blob Monster attacked, I was so scared, I forgot my own name!

Alex and I had decided to collect worms. Only purple worms — no brown ones.

That made the search more interesting.

It had rained the day before, a long, steady, spring rain. Our backyards were still soft and spongy.

The worms were coming up for air. They poked through the wet grass. And wriggled onto the driveway.

We were both crouched down, searching for purple ones — when I heard a loud, squishy sound behind me.

I spun around quickly.

And gasped when I saw the monster. "Alex — look!"

She turned too. And a whistling sound escaped her mouth. *"Wheeeeh!"* Only *this* time, she wasn't laughing.

I dropped the worm I had been carrying and took a *biiig* step back.

"It — it looks like a giant human heart!" Alex cried.

She was right.

The monster made another loud *squish* as it bounced over the grass toward us. It bounced like a giant beach ball, taller than Alex and me. Nearly as tall as the garage!

It was pink and wet. And throbbing.

BRUM BRRUUM BRUMMM. It pulsed like a heart.

It had two tiny black eyes. The eyes glowed and stared straight ahead.

On top of the pink blob, I thought I saw curled-up snakes. But as I stared in horror, I realized they weren't snakes. They were thick, purple veins — arteries tied together in a knot.

BRRUUUM BRUM BRUMM.

The monster throbbed and bounced.

"Ohhhhhh!" I groaned as I saw the sticky trail of white slime it left behind on the grass.

Alex and I were taking giant steps — backwards. We didn't want to turn our backs on the ugly thing.

"Unh unh unh!" Terrified groans escaped my throat. My heart had to be pounding at a hundred miles an hour!

I took another step back. Then another.

And as I backed away, I saw a crack open up in the creature's middle.

At first I thought the pink blob was cracking apart.

But as the crack grew wider, I realized I was staring at its mouth.

The mouth opened wider. Wider.

Wide enough to swallow a human!

4

And then a fat purple tongue plopped out. The tongue made a wet *SPLAT* as it hit the grass.

"*Ohhhhh.*" I groaned again. My stomach lurched. I nearly lost my lunch.

The end of the tongue was shaped like a shovel. A fat, sticky, purple shovel.

To shovel people into the gaping mouth?

Thick, white slime poured from the monster's mouth. "It — it's *drooling!*" I choked out.

"Run!" Alex cried.

I turned — and tripped on the edge of the driveway.

I landed hard on my elbows and knees.

And looked back — in time to see the drooling, pink mouth open wider as the tongue wrapped around me . . . pulling me, pulling me in.

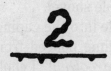

2

Alex stared at me, her mouth open wide. "Zackie, that is *awesome!*" she declared.

Adam scratched his curly, black hair and made a face. "You call that scary?" He rolled his eyes. "That's about as scary as *Goldilocks and the Three Bears.*"

I held the pages of my story in one hand. I rolled them up and took a swing at Adam with them.

He laughed and ducked out of my reach.

"That is an awesome story!" Alex repeated. "What do you call it?"

"'Adventure of the Blob Monster,'" I told her.

"Oh, wow," Adam exclaimed sarcastically. "Did you think that up all by yourself?"

Alex gave Adam a hard shove that sent him tumbling onto the couch. "Give Zackie a break," she muttered.

The three of us were hanging out in Adam's house. We were squeezed into what his parents call the rec room.

The room is so small. Only a couch and a TV fit.

It was spring vacation, and we were hanging out because we didn't know what else to do. The night before, I stayed up till midnight, working on my scary story about the Blob Monster.

I want to be a writer when I grow up. I write scary stories all the time. Then I read them to Alex and Adam.

They always react in the same way. Alex always likes my stories. She thinks they're really scary. She says that my stories are so good, they give her nightmares.

Adam always says my stories aren't scary at all. He says he can write better stories with one hand tied behind his back.

But he never does.

Adam is big and red-cheeked and chubby. He looks a little like a bear. He likes to punch people and wrestle around. Just for fun. He's actually a good guy.

He just never likes my stories.

"What's wrong with this story?" I asked him.

The three of us were crammed onto the couch now. There was nowhere else to sit.

"Stories never scare me," Adam replied. He picked an ant off the couch arm, put it between his thumb and finger, and shot it at me.

He missed.

"I thought the story was *really* scary," Alex said. "I thought you had really good description."

"I *never* get scared by books or stories," Adam insisted. "Especially stories about dumb monsters."

"Well — what *does* scare you?" Alex demanded.

"Nothing," Adam bragged. "I don't get scared by movies, either. Nothing ever scares me."

And then he opened his mouth wide in a scream of horror.

All three of us did.

We leaped off the couch — as a terrifying *screech* rang through the room.

And a black shadow swept over the floor.

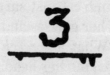

3

The shadow swooped by our feet, so fast I could barely see it.

I felt something brush my ankle. Something soft — and ghostlike.

"Whoooa!" Adam cried.

I heard hurried footsteps from the living room. Mr. Levin — Adam's dad — burst into the doorway. With his curly black hair and bearlike, round body, Mr. Levin looks a lot like Adam.

"Sorry about that!" he exclaimed. "I stepped on the cat. Did it run past here?"

We didn't answer him.

We were so stunned, we all burst out laughing.

Mr. Levin frowned at us. "I don't see what's so funny," he muttered. He spotted the cat, hiding beside the couch. He picked it up and hurried away.

The three of us dropped back onto the couch. I was still breathing hard. And I could still feel the brush of the cat on my ankle.

9

"See, Zackie?" Adam cried. He slapped me hard on the back — so hard I nearly fell off the couch. "That was a lot scarier than any story you could write."

"No way!" I insisted. "I can write a scarier story than that. The dumb cat just surprised us."

Alex pulled off her glasses and wiped the lenses on her T-shirt. "What a *screech* that cat made!" she exclaimed, shaking her head.

"I wasn't scared at all," Adam claimed. "I was just trying to scare you guys." He reached over and rubbed the palm of his hand back and forth over my head.

Don't you *hate* it when people do that?

I slugged him as hard as I could.

He only laughed.

Alex and I stayed for dinner. Mrs. Levin is a great cook. We always try to be around Adam's house at dinnertime because she always invites us to stay.

It was dark by the time Alex and I started to walk home. We'd had thunderstorms the day before and most of today. The lawns glistened from the rain. The wet street reflected the glow of street lights.

I could hear the crackle of thunder somewhere faraway. As Alex and I made our way along the sidewalk, cold rainwater dripped on us from the trees.

Adam lives on the other side of Norwood Village. But it isn't a very long walk — only about fifteen minutes.

We walked for about five minutes when we came to a row of little shops.

"Hey —!" I cried out when the antique store on the corner came into view. "It — it's been totaled!"

"It looks as if a *bomb* hit it!" Alex exclaimed.

We stayed on the corner, staring across the street at it. Part of the roof had fallen in. All the windows were shattered. One wall had nearly caved in. The shingles on the walls and the roof had been burned black.

"Was it a fire?" I wondered, leading the way across the street.

"Lightning," a woman's voice replied.

I turned to see two young women on the sidewalk beside the store. "It was struck by lightning," one of them said. "Yesterday. During the big storm. The lightning started a huge fire."

"What a mess," the other woman sighed. She pulled car keys from her pocketbook.

The two women disappeared around the corner, *tsk-tsking* about the store.

Alex and I stepped up to the front.

"Ooh, it stinks," Alex groaned, holding her nose.

"It just smells burned," I replied. I glanced down and saw that I had stepped into a deep puddle.

I jumped back.

11

"It's soaked everywhere," Alex murmured. "From the fire hoses, I guess."

A gust of wind made the front door bang.

"It's open!" I exclaimed.

The door had been taped shut. But the tape had broken off. A large yellow sign on the door declared in big black letters: DANGER — KEEP OUT.

"Alex — let's take a peek," I urged.

"No way! Zackie — stop!" Alex cried.

Too late. I was already inside.

4

I took a couple of steps into the shop and waited for my eyes to adjust to the darkness. Water dripped everywhere. An entire wall of shelves had toppled over. Broken vases, and lamps, and small statues lay scattered over the puddled floor.

"Zackie —!" Alex grabbed my shoulder. "Zackie — get *out* of here!" she whispered. "This is really dangerous."

"Leave the door open," I told her. "We need the light from the street."

"But what do you want to *see*?" Her voice echoed over the *PLUNK PLUNK PLUNK* of dripping water.

She grabbed my other arm and started to tug me out. "Come on. You saw the sign. The whole building may fall in on us."

I jerked my arm away. My sneakers squished as I walked. The carpet was soaked.

"I just want to look around for one second," I told Alex impatiently. "This is cool!"

"It isn't cool," she argued. "It's really stupid."

A row of ugly antique masks stared at us from one wall. The masks were tilted at odd angles. Other masks stared up from where they had fallen on the floor.

A tall wooden clock had its face burned black. Wooden duck decoys lay on their sides, burned and cracked.

A creaking sound overhead made me jump. I heard Alex gasp.

I raised my eyes to the ceiling. Part of it had fallen in. Was the rest about to collapse on top of us?

"Zackie — let's go!" Alex urged. She backed up toward the door. Her shoes squished over the soaked carpet.

The door banged shut behind us. I turned and saw the wind blow it back open.

PLINK PLINK. Cold water dripped onto my shoulder.

"If you don't come, I'm going without you!" Alex called. "I mean it, Zackie."

"Okay, okay," I muttered. "I'm coming. I just wanted to check out what happened."

"Hurry!" Alex urged. She was halfway out the door.

I turned and started to follow her.

But I stopped when something on a high shelf caught my eye.

"Hey, Alex —" I called. "Look!"

14

I pointed up to an old typewriter. "Wow. My dad used to have one like that when I was real little," I said.

"Zackie — I'm leaving," Alex warned.

"I *love* old typewriters!" I cried. "Look, Alex. I don't think the fire hurt it. I think it's in good shape. I just have to check it out. Okay?"

I didn't wait for her to reply.

I crossed the room. Stepped up to the shelf. Stood on tiptoe and reached for the old typewriter.

"OWWWWWWW!"

I felt a hard shock of pain. It shot through my body.

Stunned me.

Took away my breath.

Over my stunned cry, I heard the sharp *crackle* of electricity.

And I bent over — helpless — as a bright blue flame shot around my body.

5

Blue.

I saw only blue.

The deepest blue I'd ever seen.

I'm floating in the sky, I realized. I'm weightless. And I'm floating. Floating in the blue, blue sky.

The blue faded to white.

Was I still floating? Was I moving at all?

Was I *breathing*?

I struggled to speak. To shout. To make any kind of a sound.

The white faded quickly. To gray. Then black.

"Ohhhh," I heard myself moan.

Dark. So dark now. I was surrounded by darkness.

I blinked. Blinked again. And realized I was staring into the darkness of the ruined antique shop.

"Zackie? Zackie?"

I heard my name. Heard Alex repeating my name.

I cleared my throat. I sat up. My eyes darted around the store.

"Zackie? Zackie? Are you okay?"

I tried to shake my dizziness away. My whole body tingled. Tingled and hummed, as if an electrical current were running through me.

"How did I get on the floor?" I asked weakly.

Alex leaned over me, one hand on my shoulder. "You got a shock," she said, squinting hard at me through her glasses. "There must be a wire down or something."

I rubbed the back of my neck. I couldn't stop the strange tingling or the steady hum in my ears.

"Wow," I murmured.

"It was a real bad shock," Alex said softly. "I — I was so scared. You were inside a blue flame. Your whole body — it turned bright blue."

"Wow," I repeated, still fighting the dizziness.

"Your hands shot up in the air," Alex continued. "And then you bent in two. And fell to the floor. I — I thought . . ." Her voice trailed off.

PLINK PLINK.

I could hear the drip of water again. The hum in my ears had faded.

I pulled myself shakily to my feet. I stretched my arms over my head, trying to stop the strange tingling.

17

The old typewriter caught my eye again.

"Zackie — what are you doing?" Alex cried.

I moved carefully to the shelf, stepping around a puddle of water on the carpet. I took a deep breath. Stretched up on tiptoe. And pulled the old typewriter down.

"Whoa —! It weighs a ton!" I cried. "It's solid metal!"

I held it in my arms and examined it. The sleek black surface caught the glow of the streetlight outside the door. The round keys poked up toward me.

"It's awesome!" I exclaimed. "This typewriter, Alex — it's *perfect* for writing scary stories on."

"Are you *crazy*?" Alex declared. "Zackie, I think that electric shock messed up your brain!"

"But look at it!" I insisted excitedly. "It's perfect. Perfect!"

Alex rolled her eyes. "You have a brand-new computer at home," she reminded me. "And your mom gave you her old laser printer — remember?"

"I know, I know," I muttered.

"You can print eight pages a minute," Alex continued. "So what do you need a creaky old typewriter for?"

"I need it because it's perfect," I told her. "Perfect! Perfect!"

"Stop repeating that word," she snapped. "Are

you sure you're feeling okay? That was a horrible shock. Maybe I should call your parents."

"No. No, I'm fine," I insisted. The typewriter was growing heavy in my arms. "Let's just go."

Lugging the typewriter, I started to the door. But Alex blocked my path.

"You can't just *take* it!" she scolded. "It doesn't belong to you. That's stealing."

I made a face at her. "Alex, don't be dumb. Everything in this store is wrecked. Nobody will care if I take —"

I stopped with a gasp when I heard the squish of shoes on the wet carpet.

Then I heard a cough.

I turned to Alex. Caught the fear on her face. She heard the sounds too.

"Zackie, we're not alone in here," she whispered.

6

Another squishy footstep. Closer.

A chill swept down my back. I nearly dropped the typewriter.

"Hide," I whispered. I didn't need to suggest it. Alex was already slipping behind a tall display shelf.

I set the typewriter down on the floor. Then I crept behind the shelf and huddled close to Alex.

I heard another cough. And then a circle of light moved across the wet carpet. The pale yellow beam of a flashlight.

The light slid over the floor. Then it started to climb the display case. Alex and I ducked low. The circle of light washed over our heads.

My legs were trembling. I gripped the back of the case with both hands to keep myself from falling over.

"Hello?" a voice called. A woman's voice. "Hello? Is someone in here?"

Alex turned to me. She motioned with her head.

She was silently asking if we should step out and show ourselves.

I shook my head no.

How could we explain what we were doing inside the shop? How could we explain why we were hiding?

Maybe the woman will leave, I told myself. Maybe she won't find us.

Who *is* she? I wondered. Does she own the store?

I peered out around the bottom shelf. I could see the woman from the side. She was African-American. She had very short, dark hair. She wore a long raincoat.

She moved the flashlight beam along the back wall. It lit up the fallen shelf, the broken antiques.

Her footsteps slogged over the wet carpet.

"Hello?" she called. "Did someone come in here?"

I held my breath.

Please leave, I begged silently. Please don't catch us here.

The woman turned. Her light stopped on the typewriter in the middle of the floor. She kept the light steady, staring at the typewriter.

I knew what she was thinking: *How did the typewriter get on the floor?*

Slowly, she raised the light. Raised it back to the display shelf.

She stared right at us!

Could she see us hiding behind the display case?

I froze. I pretended to be a statue.

Did she see us?

No.

She muttered something to herself. The light went out.

I blinked in the sudden darkness. Her footsteps moved away.

I realized I was still holding my breath. I let it out slowly, trying not to make a sound.

Silence now. And darkness.

No footsteps. No beam of yellow light.

The front door banged shut.

Alex and I exchanged glances.

Was the woman gone? Did she leave the shop?

We didn't move.

We waited. And listened.

Silence . . .

Then Alex sneezed.

"Gotcha!" the woman cried from somewhere behind us.

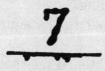

7

A hand grabbed my shoulder. Hard.

The sleeve of the raincoat brushed my face as the woman tugged me out from behind the shelf. I nearly tripped over the typewriter. The woman held me up by one arm.

Alex stepped up beside me. Her ponytail had come undone. Her blonde hair was wild around her face. She kept swallowing hard, making dry, clicking sounds with her tongue.

I guessed she was as frightened as I was.

The woman switched her flashlight on. She raised it to my face, then to Alex's.

"Were you doing some late shopping?" she demanded.

"Huh?" I managed to choke out.

"The store is closed. Couldn't you tell?" the woman snapped.

She was young and pretty. She locked her dark eyes on me.

"What are you doing in here?" she asked.

I opened my mouth to answer, but no sound came out.

"Uh . . . nothing," Alex said weakly. "We weren't doing anything."

The woman narrowed her eyes at Alex. "Then why were you hiding?"

"You f-frightened us," I stammered, finally finding my voice.

"Well, you frightened me too!" the woman exclaimed. "You frightened me plenty. I was in the back room, and . . ."

"We were walking home. We saw the store. How it was wrecked," I explained. "We just wanted to see what it looked like inside. So we came in. That's all."

The woman lowered the light to the floor. "I see," she said softly.

Her shoe made a squishing sound on the carpet. Water dripped steadily from the ceiling behind us.

"What a mess," the woman sighed. Her eyes traveled around the ruined shop. "I'm Mrs. Carter. I own this store. What's left of it."

"We — we're sorry," Alex stammered.

"You shouldn't be in here," Mrs. Carter scolded. "It's very dangerous. Some of the electrical wires are down. You didn't touch anything — did you?"

"No. Not really," Alex replied.

"Well . . . just this old typewriter," I said, gazing down at it.

24

"I *wondered* how it got down there," Mrs. Carter said. "Why did you move it?"

"I . . . like it," I told her. "It's really cool."

"Zackie writes stories," Alex told Mrs. Carter. "Scary stories."

Mrs. Carter let out a bitter laugh. "Well, you could certainly write a scary story about *this* place!"

"I'll bet I could write *awesome* scary stories on that old typewriter," I said, staring down at it.

"You want it?" Mrs. Carter asked quickly.

"Yes," I answered. "Is it for sale? How much does it cost?"

Mrs. Carter motioned with one hand. "Take it," she said.

"Excuse me?" I didn't think I'd heard her correctly.

"Go ahead. Take it," she repeated. "It's yours. For free."

"Do you mean it?" I cried excitedly. "I can have it?"

She nodded.

"Thank you!" I could feel a grin spreading over my face. "Thanks a lot!"

Mrs. Carter bent down and picked up something from the floor. "Here," she said. She handed me a fountain pen. A very old-fashioned-looking fountain pen. Heavy and black with silvery chrome on it.

"For me?" I asked, studying the pen.

Mrs. Carter nodded again. She smiled at me. "It's my Going-Out-of-Business Special Offer. You get a free pen with every typewriter."

"Wow!" I exclaimed.

Mrs. Carter moved to the door and held it open. "Now, get out of here. Both of you," she ordered. "It really is dangerous in here. I'm leaving too."

I hoisted the heavy, old typewriter into my arms. Balancing it against my chest, I followed Alex to the door.

I felt so happy! I thanked Mrs. Carter five more times. Then Alex and I said good-bye and headed for our homes.

The street was still wet. It glowed under the streetlights like a mirror. It didn't look real.

The walk home seemed to take forever. The typewriter grew heavier with each step I took.

"Weird," Alex muttered when we finally crossed onto our block.

"Huh?" I groaned. My arms were about to fall off! The typewriter weighed a *ton*!

"What's weird, Alex?"

"The way she *gave* you that valuable type-writer," Alex replied thoughtfully.

"Why is that so weird?" I demanded.

"She seemed so eager to give it away. It's almost as if she wanted to get *rid* of it," Alex said. She headed toward her house, which is next door to mine.

My knees buckled as I started up my driveway. My arms ached. My whole body ached. I struggled to hold on to the typewriter.

"That's crazy," I muttered.

Of course, I didn't know how right Alex was.

I didn't know that carrying the old typewriter home would totally ruin my life.

I dragged the typewriter into the ranch house where I live. I was gasping for breath. My arms had gone numb.

Mom and Dad were in the living room. They sat side by side on the couch, doing a crossword puzzle together.

They love crossword puzzles. I'm not sure why. Both of them are terrible spellers. They can never finish a puzzle.

Lots of times, they end up fighting about how to spell a word. Usually, they give up and rip the puzzle to pieces.

Then a few days later, they start a new one.

They both looked up as I lugged the typewriter toward my room.

"What's *that*?" Mom demanded.

"It's a typewriter," I groaned.

"I know that!" Mom protested. "I meant — where did you get it?"

"It's . . . a long story," I choked out.

Dad climbed up from the couch and hurried over to help me. "Wow. It weighs a ton," he said. "How did you ever carry it home?"

I shrugged. "It wasn't so bad," I lied.

We carried it to my room and set it down on my desk. I wanted to try it out right away. But Dad insisted that I return to the living room.

I told them the whole story. About lightning hitting the store. About going in to explore. About Mrs. Carter and how she gave me the typewriter.

I left out the part about the bad electrical shock that knocked me to the floor.

My parents are the kind of people who get upset very easily. I mean, they start yelling and screaming over crossword puzzles!

So I never tell them much. I mean, why ruin their day — or mine?

"Why do you need an old typewriter?" Mom asked, frowning at me. "No one uses typewriters anymore. You only see them in antique shops."

"I want to write my scary stories on it," I explained.

"What about your new computer?" Dad demanded. "What about the laser printer we gave you?"

"I'll use that too," I said. "You know. For schoolwork and stuff like that."

Mom rolled her eyes. "Next Zackie will be writing with a feather quill and an inkwell," she said.

They both laughed.

"Very funny," I muttered. I said good-night and hurried down the hall to my room.

I turned the corner that led to my bedroom — and stopped.

What was that strange crackling sound?

It seemed to be coming from my room. A steady, crackling buzz.

"Weird," I muttered.

I stepped into the doorway, peered into my room — and gasped!

9

"My typewriter!" I cried.

The typewriter was bathed in a bright blue glow. Blue sparks buzzed and crackled off and flew in all directions.

I stared in amazement as the blue current snapped and hummed over the typewriter.

I thought about the shock that had knocked me to the floor in the antique shop. Had the typewriter stored up some of that electricity?

No. That was impossible.

But then why was the typewriter glowing under a crackling, blue current now?

"Mom! Dad!" I called. "Come here! You have to see this!"

They didn't reply.

I hurtled down the hall to the living room. "Quick! Come quick!" I shouted. "You won't believe this!"

They had returned to their crossword puzzle. Dad glanced up as I burst into the room. "How do

31

you spell 'peregrine'?" he asked. "It's a kind of falcon."

"Who cares?" I cried. "My typewriter — it's going to blow up or something!"

That got them off the couch.

I led the way, running full speed down the hall. They followed close behind.

I stopped at my doorway and pointed to my desk. "Look —!" I cried.

All three of us peered across the room.

At the typewriter. The black metal typewriter with its black roller and rows of black keys ringed with silver.

No blue.

No blue electrical current. No sparks. No crackle or buzz.

Just an old typewriter sitting on a desk.

"Funny joke," Dad muttered, rolling his eyes at me.

Mom shook her head. "I don't know where Zackie gets his sense of humor. Not from *my* side of the family."

"Your side of the family doesn't need a sense of humor. They're *already* a joke!" Dad snapped.

They walked off arguing.

I edged slowly, carefully, into my room. I crept up to the typewriter.

I reached out a hand. I lowered it toward the typewriter.

Lowered it until it was less than an inch away.

Then I stopped.
My hand started to shake.
I stared down at the solid, dark machine.
Should I touch it?
Would it shock me again?
Slowly . . . slowly, I lowered my hand.

10

Alex slammed her locker shut. She adjusted her backpack and turned to me. "So what happened? Did the typewriter zap you?"

It was the next morning. Spring vacation was over. School had started again.

I had hurried down the hall to our lockers to tell Alex the whole typewriter story. I knew she was the only person in the world who would believe me.

"No. It didn't zap me," I told her. "I touched it, and nothing happened. I pushed down some of the keys. I turned the roller. Nothing happened."

Alex stared hard at me. "Nothing?"

"Nothing."

"That isn't a very good story," she teased. "It has a very weak ending."

I laughed. "Do you think it would be a better ending if I got fried?"

"Much better," she replied.

It was late. The first bell had already rung. The hall was nearly empty.

"I'm going to rewrite the Blob Monster story," I told her. "I have a lot of new ideas. I can't wait to start working on it."

She turned to me. "On the old typewriter?"

I nodded. "I'm going to make the story longer — and scarier. That old typewriter is so weird. I *know* it's going to help me write scarier than ever!" I exclaimed.

I heard giggling.

I spun around and saw Emmy and Annie Bell. They're twins, and they're in our class. Adam came trailing after them. He punched me in the shoulder — so hard, I bounced against the lockers.

Emmy and Annie are good friends with Adam. But not with Alex and me.

They both have curly red hair, lots of freckles, and lots of dimples. The only way to tell Emmy from Annie is to ask, "Which one are you?"

Emmy grinned at me. I mean, I *think* it was Emmy. "Do you really believe in monsters?" she asked.

They both giggled again, as if Emmy had asked something really funny.

"Maybe," I replied. "But I wasn't talking about real monsters. I was talking about a scary story I'm writing."

And then I added nastily, "You two wouldn't understand — since you haven't learned to write yet!"

"Ha-ha," they both said sarcastically. "You're so funny, Zackie."

"Funny-looking!" Adam added. The oldest joke in the universe.

"But *do* you believe in monsters?" Emmy insisted.

"Adam says you do," her sister added. "Adam says you think a monster lives under your bed!"

"I do not!" I screamed.

They both giggled.

"Adam is a liar!" I cried. I tried to grab him, but he dodged away from me, laughing his head off.

"Zackie sees monsters everywhere," Adam teased, grinning at Emmy and Annie. "He thinks when he opens his locker door, a monster will jump out at him."

They giggled again.

"Give me a break," I muttered. "We're going to be late."

I turned away from their grinning faces. I turned the lock on my locker and pulled open the door.

Then I knelt down to pull out my books.

And something leaped out of my locker!

I saw a white flash.

"Huh?" I cried out in surprise.

Another one jumped out.

And then I gasped when something plopped onto my head.

Something *alive*!

I fell to my knees. Reached up to grab for it.

I felt its claws tangle in my hair.

"Help!" I cried. "Help me!"

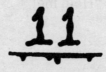

11

The creature moved across my head.

And dropped down the back of my shirt!

Its hot body slid down my skin. Its claws prickled and pinched.

"Help me! Help!" I jumped up, kicking and stomping and squirming.

I frantically slapped at my back.

Adam stepped up to me. He grabbed me by the shoulders. Then he tugged open the back of my shirt.

And plucked the creature off my back.

He held his hand in front of my face. "Wow! What a monster!" he exclaimed. "That's *scaaaaaary!*"

Still trembling, I stared at the creature.

A white mouse.

A little white mouse.

Emmy and Annie were doubled over beside Adam, laughing their heads off.

Even Alex was laughing. Great friend, huh?

"Zackie, I guess you really *do* see monsters

everywhere!" Annie exclaimed. "Even teeny white ones!"

That got them all laughing again.

"Did you see that awesome dance he did?" Adam asked. Adam did an imitation of my frantic dance. He slapped at his head and neck and stomped wildly on the floor.

"Excellent!" Emmy and Annie declared together.

They all laughed again.

Alex stopped laughing and stepped up beside me. She brushed something off my shoulder.

"Mouse hair," she murmured.

Then she turned to the others. "We should give Zackie a break," she told them. "Someday he's going to be a famous horror writer."

"Someday he's going to be a famous *chicken*!" Annie exclaimed.

Emmy made clucking sounds and flapped her elbows.

"Do you believe it? The famous horror writer is afraid of *mice*!" Adam cried.

Emmy and Annie thought that was really funny. Their red hair bobbed up and down as they laughed.

Emmy glanced at her watch — and gasped. "We're really late!"

She and her sister spun around and ran down the hall. Adam put the mouse in his pocket and went tearing after them.

I knelt down to pull my books from the bottom of my locker. I reached in carefully. I had to make sure there were no more mice.

Alex stood over me. "You okay?" she asked softly.

"Go away," I snapped.

"What did *I* do?" Alex demanded.

"Just go away," I muttered.

I didn't want her around. I didn't want anyone around.

I felt like a total jerk.

Why did I let little mice scare me like that? Why did I have to freak out in front of everyone?

Because I'm a total jerk, I decided.

I shoved books and a Trapper Keeper into my backpack. Then I stood up and started to close my locker.

Alex leaned against the wall. "I told you to go away," I snapped at her again.

She started to reply, but stopped when Mr. Conklin, the principal, turned the corner.

Mr. Conklin is a tall, pencil-thin man, with a narrow, red face and big ears that stick out like jug handles. He talks really fast. Always runs instead of walking. And always seems to be moving in eight directions at once.

He eyed Alex, then me. "Who let the mice out of the science lab?" he demanded breathlessly.

"Th-they were in Zackie's locker —" Alex started.

Before she could explain the rest, Mr. Conklin narrowed his eyes at me. His face grew even redder.

"Zackie, I'd like to see you in my office," he ordered. "Right now."

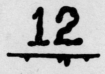

12

I didn't say much at dinner.

I kept wondering if I should tell Mom and Dad about my adventures at school that day. But I decided to keep silent.

I didn't need them laughing at me too.

And I didn't need them asking a million questions about what Mr. Conklin said to me.

He had been pretty nice about it, actually. He just warned me to try to keep live creatures out of my locker.

After dinner, Dad and I loaded the dishwasher and cleaned up. I was sponging off the dinner table when Alex appeared. "How's it going?" she asked. "Did Mr. Conklin —"

I slapped a hand over her mouth to shut her up.

I could see Mom and Dad watching from the other room. "What about Mr. Conklin?" Mom demanded.

"He's a nice guy," I replied.

I dragged Alex to the den. "So? How's it going?" she repeated.

"How's it going?" I cried shrilly. "How's it going? How can you ask me 'how's it going'?"

"Well . . ." she started.

"It's going *terrible*!" I cried. "I had the *worst* day! Kids were laughing at me all day. Everywhere I went, kids made mouse faces at me and squeaked at me."

She started to smile, but cut it off.

"I don't know why I lost it like that this morning," I continued. "I felt so dumb. I —"

"It was just a joke," Alex interrupted. "No big deal."

"Easy for you to say," I grumbled. "You didn't have a hundred disgusting rodents crawling all over your body."

"A hundred?" Alex said. "How about *one*?"

"It seemed like a hundred," I mumbled. I decided to change the subject. "Look at this," I said.

I walked over to the desk by the window. After school, I had worked there for three hours. I picked up a stack of pages.

"What are those?" Alex asked, following me to the desk.

"My new Blob Monster story," I replied, holding up the handwritten pages. "I'm making it even scarier."

Alex took the pages from my hand and shuffled

through them. Then she narrowed her eyes at me. "You didn't type them on the old typewriter?"

"Of course not." I took the pages back. "I always write the first draft by hand. I don't type my stories until I've got them just right."

I picked up the pen from the desk. "I used the antique pen that woman gave me in the shop," I told Alex. "What a great pen. It writes so smoothly. I can't believe she gave it to me for free!"

Alex laughed. "You're such a weird guy, Zackie. You get so excited about things like pens and typewriters." And then she added, "I think that's cool."

I glanced over my story. "Now it's time to type it," I said. "I'm so excited. I can't wait to use the old typewriter."

I led the way into my room. I was halfway to my desk when I stopped.

And let out a startled cry.

The typewriter was gone.

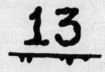

13

Alex and I both gaped at the empty spot on the front of my desktop. Alex pushed up her glasses and squinted.

"It — it's gone," I murmured weakly. My knees started to buckle. I grabbed my dresser to hold myself up.

"Weird," Alex muttered, shaking her head. "Are you sure —"

"It just disappeared into thin air!" I interrupted. "I don't *believe* this! How? How could it disappear?"

"How could *what* disappear?" a voice called from the doorway.

I whirled around — to see Dad lumber heavily into the room. He carried the old typewriter in his arms.

"Dad — why . . . ?" I started.

He set it down on the desk. Then he pushed his curly black hair off his forehead and grinned at me. "I cleaned it for you, Zackie," he said. "And put in a new ribbon."

He wiped sweat off his forehead with the back of his hand. "Ribbons are hard to find these days," he added. "No one uses typewriters anymore."

Alex laughed. "Zackie thought the typewriter disappeared into thin air!"

I flashed Alex an angry look. "Alex — give me a break," I whispered.

She made a face at me.

Dad shook his head. "It's a little too heavy to disappear into thin air," he sighed. "It weighs a ton! More than a computer!"

I walked over to the typewriter and ran my hand over the smooth, dark metal. "Thanks for cleaning it up, Dad," I said. "It looks awesome."

"A few of the keys were sticking," Dad added. "So I oiled them up. I think the old machine is working fine now, Zackie. You should be able to write some great stories on it."

"Thanks, Dad," I repeated.

I couldn't wait to get started. I reached into my top drawer for some paper. Then I noticed that Dad hadn't left. He was lingering by the door, watching Alex and me.

"Your mom went across the street to visit Janet Hawkins, our new neighbor," he said. "It's such a beautiful spring night. I thought maybe you two would like to take a walk into town to get some ice cream."

"Uh . . . no thanks," Alex replied. "I already had dessert at home. Before I came over."

"And I really want to get started typing my new scary story," I told him.

He sighed and looked disappointed. I think he really wanted an excuse to get ice cream.

As soon as he left, I dropped into my desk chair. I slid a fresh, white sheet of paper into the typewriter roller.

Alex pulled up a chair and sat beside me. "Can I try the typewriter after you?" she asked.

"Yes. *After* me," I replied impatiently.

I really wanted to get my story typed.

I let my eyes wander over the round, black keys. Then I leaned forward and started to type.

Typing on a typewriter is a lot different from typing on a keyboard. For one thing, you have to press the keys a lot harder.

It took me a few tries to get the feel of the thing. Then I typed the first words of the story:

IT WAS A DARK AND STORMY NIGHT.

"Hey —!" I uttered a cry as lightning flashed in my bedroom window.

Rain pounded on the glass.

A sharp roar of thunder shook the house.

Darkness swept over me as all the lights went out.

"Zackie —?" Alex cried in a tiny voice. "Zackie? Zackie? Are you all right?"

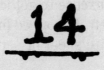

14

I swallowed hard. "Yes. I'm okay," I said quietly.

Alex is the only person in the world who knows that I'm afraid of the dark.

I'm afraid of mice. And I'm afraid of the dark. I admit it.

And I'm afraid of a lot of other things.

I'm afraid of big dogs. I'm afraid of going down to the basement when I'm all alone in the house. I'm afraid of jumping into the deep end of the swimming pool.

I've told Alex about some of my fears. But not all of them.

I mean, it's kind of embarrassing.

Why do I write scary stories if I'm afraid of so many things?

I don't know. Maybe I write better stories because I know what being scared feels like.

"The lights went off so suddenly," Alex said. She stood beside me, leaning over my desk to see out the window. "Usually they flicker or some-thing."

Sheets of rain pounded against the windowpane. Jagged streaks of lightning crackled across the sky.

I stayed in my desk chair, gripping the arms tightly. "I'm glad Adam isn't here," I murmured. "He'd just make fun of me."

"But you're not very scared now — are you?" Alex asked.

An explosion of thunder made me nearly jump out of the chair.

"A little," I confessed.

And then I heard the footsteps. Heavy, thudding footsteps from out in the hall.

Thunder roared again.

I spun away from the window. And listened to the footsteps, thudding heavily on the carpet.

"Who's there?" I called through the darkness.

I saw a flicker of yellow light in the doorway. A shadow swept over the wallpaper in the hall.

Dad stepped into the room. "This is so weird," he said. He was carrying two candles in candle-sticks. Their flames bent and nearly went out as he carried them to my desk.

"Where did that storm come from?" Dad asked, setting the candles beside my typewriter. "Are you okay, Zackie?"

I forgot. Dad also knows I'm scared of the dark.

"I'm fine," I told him. "Thanks for the candles."

Dad stared out the window. We couldn't really see anything out there. The rain was coming down too hard.

"The sky was clear a few seconds ago," Dad said, leaning over me to get a better view. "I can't believe such a big storm could blow in so quickly."

"It's weird," I agreed.

We stared at the rain for a minute or so. Sheets of lightning made the backyard glow like silver.

"I'm going to call your mother," Dad said. "I'm going to tell her to wait out the storm." He patted me on the back, then headed to the door.

"Don't you want a candle?" I called after him.

"No. I'll find my way," he replied. "I have a flashlight in the basement." He disappeared down the hall.

"What do you want to do now?" Alex asked. Her face looked orange in the candlelight. Her eyes glowed like cat eyes.

I turned back to the typewriter. "It would be cool to write by candlelight," I said. "Scary stories should *always* be written by candlelight. I'll bet that's how all the famous horror writers write their stories."

"Cool," Alex replied. "Go ahead."

I slid the candlesticks closer. The yellow light flickered over the typewriter keys.

I leaned forward and read over the first sentence of my story:

IT WAS A DARK AND STORMY NIGHT.

Then I hit the space bar and typed the next sentence:

THE WIND BEGAN TO HOWL.

I hit the space bar again. And raised my fingers to type the next sentence.

But a rattling noise made me jump.

"What is *that*?" I gasped.

"The window." Alex pointed.

Outside, the wind blew hard, rattling the windowpane.

Over the steady roar of the rain, I heard another sound. A strange howl.

I gripped the arms of my desk chair. "Do you hear that?" I asked Alex.

She nodded. Her eyes squinted out the window.

"It's just the wind," she said softly. "It's howling through the trees."

Outside, the howling grew louder as the wind swirled around my house. The window rattled and shook.

The howling grew high and shrill, almost like a human voice, a human wail.

I felt a chill run down my back.

Gripping the chair arms tightly, I struggled to keep my fear down.

It's just a storm, I told myself. Just a rainstorm. Just a lot of rain and wind.

I glanced at the words I had typed. In the flickering, orange light, the black type jumped out at me:

THE WIND BEGAN TO HOWL.

I listened to the shrill howl outside. It seemed to surround me, surround the house.

"How strange," I muttered.

And then, things got a lot stranger.

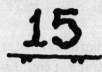

15

"You're not getting very far with the story," Alex said.

"Well, the storm —" I started.

She put a hand on my shoulder. "You're shaking!" she exclaimed.

"No, I'm not!" I lied.

"Yes, you are. You're shaking," she insisted.

"No way. I'm okay. Really," I said, trying to keep my voice calm and steady. "I'm not that afraid, Alex."

"Maybe if you work on the story, you won't think about the storm so much," she suggested.

"Right. The story," I agreed.

An explosion of thunder shook the house.

I let out a sharp cry. "Why does it seem so close?" I exclaimed. "The lightning and thunder — it sounds as if it's all right in the backyard!"

Alex grabbed my shoulders and turned me to the typewriter. "Type," she ordered. "Pretend there is no storm. Just type."

I obediently raised my hands to the keys of the old typewriter. The candles had burned down a little, and the page was shadowy and dark.

I typed the next sentence:

ALEX AND ZACKIE WERE ALONE IN THE DARK HOUSE, LISTENING TO THE STORM.

Rain pounded hard against the window. In a white flash of lightning, I could see the trees in the backyard, bending and trembling in the howling wind.

"The story is about *us*?" Alex asked, leaning over my shoulder to read what I had typed.

"Of course," I replied. "You know that I always write about us and the other kids at school. It makes it easier to describe everyone."

"Well, don't let the Blob Monster eat me!" she instructed. "I want to be the hero. Not the dinner!"

I laughed.

A crash of thunder made me jump.

I turned back to the typewriter. I squinted to read over the sentences I had typed.

"The candles aren't giving enough light," I complained. "How did writers *do* it in the old days? They must have all gone blind!"

"Let's go and get more candles," Alex suggested.

"Good idea," I agreed.

We each picked up a candlestick. Holding them in front of us, we made our way down the hall.

The candles bent and flickered. Our footsteps

were drowned out by the steady roar of rain on the roof.

"Dad?" I called. "Hey, Dad — we need more candles!"

No reply.

We stepped into the living room. Two candles glowed on the mantelpiece. Two more stood side by side on the coffee table in front of the couch.

"Dad?" I called. "Where are you?"

Holding our candles high, Alex and I made our way to the den. Then the kitchen. Then Mom and Dad's bedroom.

No Dad.

Holding my candle tightly in one hand, I pulled open the door to the basement. "Dad? Are you down there?"

Silence.

I felt another tingling chill run down my back. I turned to Alex. "He — he's gone!" I stammered. "We're all alone!"

16

"He *has* to be here," Alex insisted. "Why would he go out in this storm?"

"For ice cream?" I suggested. "He really wanted some ice cream."

Alex frowned. "Your dad would go out in this storm to get a cup of ice cream? That's impossible."

"You don't know my dad!" I replied.

"He's here," Alex insisted. She set down the candle and cupped her hands around her mouth. "Mr. Beauchamp? Mr. Beauchamp?" she called.

No reply.

Wind howled outside the living-room window. Lightning flickered.

"Hey —!" I cried.

In the flash of bright light, I saw a car in the driveway. Dad's car.

I made my way to the window and peered out. "Dad didn't drive anywhere," I told Alex. "His car is still here. And he wouldn't walk."

"Mr. Beauchamp? Mr. Beauchamp?" Alex tried again.

"Weird," I muttered. "He wouldn't go out without telling us — would he? He — he just disappeared."

Alex's eyes flashed. Her expression changed. She narrowed her eyes at me.

"What's wrong?" I asked. "Why are you staring at me like that?"

"Zackie — what was the last sentence you typed?" she demanded, still squinting at me.

"Huh?"

"In your story," she said impatiently. "What was the last sentence?"

I thought hard. Then I recited it:

"ALEX AND ZACKIE WERE ALONE IN THE DARK HOUSE, LISTENING TO THE STORM."

Alex nodded her head solemnly.

"So what?" I asked. "What does the story have to do with anything?"

"Don't you see?" Alex replied. "You wrote that we were all alone in the house — and now we're *all alone*!"

I stared back at her. I still didn't know what she was talking about.

"Zackie — this is amazing!" she cried. "What is the *first* sentence of the story?"

I told it to her:

"IT WAS A DARK AND STORMY NIGHT."

"Yes!" Alex cried excitedly. Her eyes went wide. The candle shook in her hand. "Yes! A dark and stormy night! But it had been a nice night — right?"

"Huh?" I struggled to follow her.

"Your dad said there wasn't a cloud in the sky. Remember? That's why he wanted to walk into town."

"Yeah. Right. So what?" I demanded.

She let out an impatient sigh. "So then you typed that it was dark and stormy — and guess what? It became dark and stormy."

"But, Alex —" I started.

She raised a finger to her lips to silence me. "And then you typed that we were all alone in the dark house. And that came true too!"

"Oh, no!" I groaned. "You're not going to tell me that my story is coming true — are you?"

"So far it has," she insisted. "Every word of it."

"That's really dumb," I told her. "I think this storm has freaked you out more than me!"

"Then how else do you explain it?" Alex shot back.

"Explain it? A big rainstorm came up. That's how I explain it."

I picked up a candlestick from the mantel. Now I had one in each hand. I started back to my room.

Alex followed me. "How do you explain your dad disappearing into thin air?"

Our shadows edged along the wall, bending in the flickering light. I wished the electricity would come back on.

I stepped into my room. "Dad didn't disappear. He went out," I told Alex. I sighed. "Your idea is crazy. Just because I typed that it was stormy out . . ."

"Let's test it," Alex urged.

"Excuse me?"

She dragged me to the desk chair. She pushed me into it.

"Hey —" I protested. "I almost dropped the candles."

"Type something," Alex instructed. "Go ahead, Zackie. Type something — and we'll see if it comes true."

17

The wind howled outside the house, rattling the windowpane. I set my candles down, one on each side of the old typewriter.

I leaned forward and read the story so far.

Alex was right.

Everything I had typed had come true.

But her idea was totally dumb.

"Type!" she ordered, standing behind me, her hands on my shoulders.

I glanced back at her. "Alex — haven't you ever heard of *coincidence*?"

"Oooh — big word!" she replied sarcastically. "Are you sure you're ready for such a big word?"

I ignored her remark. "A coincidence is when two things happen by accident," I explained. "For example, I type that it's stormy out — and then it starts to storm. That's called a coincidence."

She shoved me toward the typewriter. "Prove

it," she insisted. "Go ahead, Zackie. Type the next sentence, and let's see if it comes true."

She squeezed my shoulders. And then added, "Or are you *chicken*?"

I wriggled out from under her hands. "Okay, okay," I groaned. "I'll prove just how dumb you are."

I reached for the handwritten pages of the story. And I found the next sentence.

Then I raised my hands to the old typewriter keyboard and typed it in:

THEY HEARD A KNOCK ON THE DOOR.

I lowered my hands to my lap. And sat back.

"See?" I sneered. "Any more bright ideas?"

Then I heard a knock on the door!

I gasped.

Alex let out a startled cry.

"That didn't h-happen," I stammered. "I didn't hear that. I imagined it."

"But we *both* heard it," Alex replied, her eyes wide. "We *both* couldn't imagine it!"

"But it's *impossible*!" I insisted. I picked up a candle. Then I jumped up from the desk chair and hurried across the bedroom.

"Where are you going?" Alex demanded, chasing after me.

"To answer the door," I told her.

"No —!" she gasped.

I was already jogging through the dark hall. My

heart pounded. The candle flame seemed to throb in rhythm with my heart.

I glanced back and saw Alex running after me. "Zackie — wait!"

I didn't stop. I ran to the front door.

"No! Please — don't open it!" Alex pleaded.

"I have to," I told her. "We have to see who's there."

"Zackie — don't!" Alex begged.

But I ignored her. And pulled open the door.

18

Alex gasped.

I stared out into the rain.

No one there.

No one.

Rain pattered the front stoop. The big raindrops bounced like balls in every direction.

I pushed the door shut. And brushed a cold raindrop off my forehead.

"Weird," Alex muttered, tugging at her blonde ponytail. She pushed her glasses up on her nose. "Weird."

"It had to be a tree branch," I said. "The wind blew a tree branch against the door. That's all."

"No way," Alex insisted. "Tree branches don't *knock*. I heard a knock on the door — and so did you."

We stared at each other for a long moment. Then we stared at the door.

"I know!" Alex declared. Behind her glasses,

her eyes flashed excitedly. "I know why there was no one at the door!"

"I *don't* want to know!" I groaned. "I don't want to hear any more crazy ideas about my story coming true."

"But don't you see?" she cried. "There was no one at the door because you didn't *write* someone at the door!"

"*AAAAAGGH!*" I screamed. "Alex, please — give me a break. You don't really believe that I am controlling everything that happens — do you?"

She twisted her face, thinking hard.

"No," she finally replied.

"Good!" I exclaimed.

"I think the old *typewriter* is controlling everything," she said.

"Alex — go lie down," I instructed. "I'm calling your parents to come get you. You are *sick*. Definitely sick."

She ignored me. "Maybe that's why the woman in the burned-out shop gave you the typewriter," she continued. "Maybe she knew it had strange powers. And she couldn't wait to get rid of it."

"I can't wait to get rid of *you*!" I snapped. "Alex, please tell me you're not serious. You're scaring me with this nutty talk. Really."

"But, Zackie, I'm right. Everything you type — it comes true!" Alex grabbed my arm and started to pull me down the hall.

I pulled back. "Where are you taking me?" I demanded.

"One more test," she insisted.

I followed her into my room. "One more?" I asked. "One more test — and then you'll shut up about this?"

She raised her right hand. "Promise." She lowered her hand. "But, you'll see, Zackie. You'll see that I'm not crazy. Whatever you type on that old typewriter comes true."

I sat down at the desk and slid the candles closer to the typewriter. I stared into the flickering orange light, reading the words of the story.

"Hurry up," Alex urged. "Type that someone is standing on the other side of the door."

"Okay, okay," I muttered. "But this is crazy." I raised my hands to the old typewriter keys and typed:

DRENCHED WITH RAIN, ADAM STOOD ON THE FRONT PORCH.

I lowered my hands to my lap.

I listened for a knock on the front door.

But all I heard was the steady rush of the wind and the patter of rain against the house.

I waited, listening hard.

No knock.

I realized I was holding my breath. I let it out slowly, listening. Listening.

"No knock," I told Alex. I couldn't keep a grin

from spreading across my face. A triumphant grin. "See? It didn't work."

She frowned. She leaned over my shoulder and read the words again. "Of *course* it didn't work," she said. "You didn't write that Adam knocked. You put him on the porch. But you didn't make him knock."

I sighed. "Okay. If it will make you happy . . ."

I turned back to the typewriter and typed:

ADAM KNOCKED ON THE FRONT DOOR.

As I lowered my hands from the keys, I heard a loud knock on the front door.

"See?" Alex cried. It was her turn to grin.

"This *can't* be happening!" I gasped.

We didn't bother with candles. We both ran full speed through the hall to the front door.

Alex reached it first. She grabbed the knob and pulled open the door.

"Is it really Adam?" I called.

19

I gaped in shock as Alex pulled Adam in from the rain.

He was drenched! His curly black hair was matted to his forehead. He wasn't wearing a rain slicker or jacket. His soaked T-shirt stuck to his body.

"Whoooa!" he exclaimed, shivering. He wrapped his arms around his chubby body as if trying to warm himself.

Water poured off him and puddled on the floor.

"Adam —!" I opened my mouth to say something — but I was too shocked to form words.

"It — it's *true!*" Alex stammered. "It really works!"

"Huh?" Adam appeared dazed.

"What are you doing here?" I demanded, feeling dazed myself.

His eyes wandered around the living room. "I'm not sure!" he exclaimed. "I — I know I came here for a reason. But I don't remember what it is."

"Zackie *made* you come here!" Alex declared.

Adam shook his head hard, shaking water off himself like a dog. He narrowed his eyes at Alex. "Excuse me?"

Alex studied Adam. "Did you stand on the front porch for a while before you knocked?" she demanded.

Adam nodded. "Yeah. I did! I'm not sure why. I just stood there. I guess I was trying to remember why I came over here. How did you know that?"

Alex grinned at me. "See? I was right all along."

I swallowed hard. My head was spinning. "Yes. You were right," I murmured.

The old typewriter . . .

Whatever I typed on it came true.

"What's going on?" Adam demanded impatiently. He shook more water onto the rug. "Why are we in the dark?"

"The storm knocked out the lights," I told him. "Follow me."

I led the way to my room. On the way, I stopped at the linen closet and gave Adam a bath towel. He dried himself off as we walked to my room.

I couldn't wait to tell him about my amazing typewriter. "You're not going to believe this!" I started.

I took him over to the typewriter. He stared at it in the orange candlelight.

Then Alex and I told him the whole story.

When we finished, Adam burst out laughing. "Very funny," he said.

He shook his head. His curly hair was still soaked. Water dripped down his forehead.

"I know you want to pay me back, Zackie," he said. "I know you want to pay me back for putting the mice in your locker. I know I embarrassed you in school."

He put a moist hand on my shoulder. "But there is no way I'm going to fall for a dumb story like that. No way."

"Zackie will prove it to you," Alex chimed in.

Adam sneered and rolled his eyes. "I can hardly wait."

"No. Really," I insisted. "It's not a joke, Adam. It's real. Come here. I'll show you."

I pulled him up to the desk. Then I dropped into the chair and quickly typed the next lines of my scary story:

THE STORM STOPPED SUDDENLY. ALL WAS QUIET. TOO QUIET.

Adam and Alex read the words over my shoulder.

I jumped up and pulled Adam to the window. "Go ahead. Check it out," I urged.

20

All three of us slid around my desk and pressed our faces to the window.

"Yes!" I cried, shaking my fists above my head. "Yes!"

The rain had stopped.

I edged between my two friends and pushed up the window. "Listen," I instructed.

We all listened.

Not a sound outside. Not even the drip of rain from the trees. Not even a whisper of wind.

"Yes!" Alex cried happily. She and I slapped a high five.

I turned to Adam. "Do you see?" I cried. "Do you believe us now?"

"Do you see?" Alex repeated.

Adam backed away from the window. "See *what*?" he demanded. "Do I see that the rain has stopped? Yes. I see it."

"But — but —" I pointed to the typewriter.

Adam laughed. "Have you both *lost* it?" he cried.

"Do you really think *you* stopped the rain? You two are *totally* messed up!"

"It's true!" I insisted. "Adam, I just proved it to you."

He laughed and rolled his eyes.

I wanted to punch his laughing face. I really did.

Here was the most amazing thing that ever happened to anyone in the history of the world — and he thought it was a big joke!

I grabbed his arm. "Here," I said breathlessly. "I'll prove it again. Watch."

I dragged him to the typewriter.

I didn't bother to sit down. I leaned over the desk and started to type something.

But before I had typed two words, Alex tugged me away.

"What are you *doing*?" I cried. I struggled to break away. But she pulled me out to the hall.

"He's not going to believe us, Zackie," she whispered. "You can prove it to him a dozen times, and he won't believe it."

"Of course he will!" I insisted. "He'll —"

"No way," Alex interrupted. "Go ahead. Type ADAM HAS TWO HEADS. If you do it, *both* of his heads won't believe you!"

I had to think about that one.

"One more try," I said. "Let me type one more sentence. When Adam sees it come true, maybe he'll change his mind. Maybe he'll see it isn't a joke."

Alex shrugged. "Go ahead. But he has his mind made up, Zackie. He thinks you're trying to pay him back for the mice in your locker."

"One more try," I insisted.

I glanced into the room. "No —! Adam — stop!" I shrieked.

He had his back turned to us. But I could see that he was leaning over the typewriter.

He was typing something onto the page!

"Adam — stop!" Alex and I both wailed.

We dove into the room.

He spun around, a wide grin on his face. "I've got to go!" he exclaimed.

He swept past us and out into the hall. "So long, suckers!" he called. He disappeared down the hall.

I hurtled to the desk. My heart pounding, I stared down at the typewriter.

What did Adam type?

21

I heard the front door slam. Adam had run out of the house.

I didn't care about Adam now. I only cared about one thing.

What did he type on the old typewriter?

I grabbed the sheet of paper — and pulled it from the roller. Then I held it close to a candle flame to read it.

"Careful! You'll set it on fire!" Alex warned.

I moved it back from the flame. Orange light flickered over the page. My hand was trembling so hard, I struggled to read it.

"Well? What did he type?" Alex asked impatiently.

"He — he — he —" I sputtered.

She grabbed the paper from my hand and read Adam's sentence out loud:

"THE BLOB MONSTER HID IN ZACKIE'S BASEMENT, WAITING FOR FRESH MEAT."

"What a jerk!" I cried. "I don't believe him! Why did he type that on my story?"

Alex stared unhappily at the page. "He thought it was funny."

"Ha-ha," I said weakly. I grabbed the page back from her. "He ruined my story. Now I have to start it all over again."

"Forget your story. What about the Blob Monster?" Alex cried.

"Huh?" A chill tightened the back of my neck. The sheet of paper slipped from my hand.

"Everything typed on the old typewriter comes true," Alex murmured.

I was so upset about Adam ruining my story that I had forgotten!

"You mean —?" I started. My mouth suddenly felt very dry.

"There is a Blob Monster waiting in the basement," Alex said in a low whisper. "Waiting for fresh meat."

"Fresh meat," I repeated. I gulped.

Alex and I froze for a moment, staring at each other in the darting candlelight.

"But there is no such thing as a Blob Monster," I said finally. "I made it up. So how can a Blob Monster be hiding in my basement?"

Alex's eyes flashed behind her glasses. "You're right!" she cried. "They don't exist! So . . . no problem!" She smiled.

But her smile faded when we heard a noise.

A heavy *THUD THUD*.

I gasped. "What was *that*?"

We both turned to the door.

And heard the sound again. *THUD THUD*.

Heavy and slow. Like footsteps.

"Is it . . . is it coming from the b-b-b-?" I was so scared I was stuttering.

Alex nodded. "The basement," she whispered, finishing the word for me.

I picked up a candlestick. The light bounced over the wall and floor. I couldn't stop my hand from shaking.

Holding it in front of me, I made my way into the hall.

Alex huddled close, keeping with me step for step.

THUD THUD.

We both stopped. The sounds were closer. Louder.

Taking a deep breath, I stepped up to the basement door.

Alex hung back, her hands pressed to her face. Behind her glasses, her eyes were wide with fear.

THUD THUD.

"It's coming up the stairs!" I cried. "Run!"

Too late.

I heard another *THUD* — and the door crashed open.

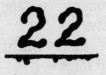

22

A beam of white light made me shut my eyes.

My hands shot up to shield myself.

Behind the beam of light, a large, dark figure lumbered heavily through the door.

"Dad!" I gasped.

My dad lowered the flashlight to the floor.

"Dad! What were you *doing* down there?" I demanded in a high, shrill voice.

"Are you two okay?" Dad asked, narrowing his eyes at us. "Why do you look so frightened?"

"We . . . uh . . . well . . ." I didn't know how to explain. I *couldn't* tell him we thought he was a Blob Monster!

Dad pointed to the basement with the flashlight. "I've been down there checking the circuit breakers," he explained. "I can't figure out why the lights haven't come back on." He scratched his head.

"We were looking for you," Alex said. "We shouted down to the basement for you."

"I went across the street to check on your mother. Then I went into the back room of the basement," Dad replied. "I guess I couldn't hear you."

He shook his head. "What a strange storm. It came up so suddenly. And then it just stopped. As if someone turned it on, then turned it off."

Alex and I glanced at each other. "Yes. It was weird," Alex agreed.

I took a deep breath. "Uh . . . Dad?" I started.

He beamed the light at my feet. "Yes, Zackie?"

"Dad . . . when you were down in the basement . . . was there anything else down there with you?"

His heavy eyebrows rose up on his forehead. He stared hard at me. "Excuse me?"

"Did you see anything strange down there? Or hear anything strange?"

He shook his head. "No. Nothing." His eyes locked on mine. "Are you afraid, Zackie? I know you have problems with being in the dark like this. Would you like to hang out with me for a while?"

"No. I'm fine. Really," I insisted. "I just wondered . . ."

Dad stepped past us and started toward the kitchen. "I'm going to call the electric company," he said. "They should have fixed the lines by now."

I watched him make his way down the hall. The white beam of light bounced in front of him.

I held my candle up to the basement door. "I

77

guess the typewriter didn't work this time," I told Alex happily. "No Blob Monster."

"Let's go downstairs and check it out!" she replied.

"Huh?" I backed away from the open doorway. "Are you crazy?"

"We have to know if the old typewriter has powers or not," Alex said. "We have no choice, Zackie. We have to check out the basement."

"But — but —"

She pushed past me onto the basement stairway. She walked down the first two steps.

Then she turned back to me. "Are you coming with me, or not?"

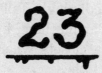

23

Did I have a choice?

No.

For one thing, I had the candle. I couldn't let Alex go down there by herself — in total darkness.

But I held back, my heart pounding, my mouth dry as cotton. "Dad said he didn't hear anything," I said. "So there is no reason for us to go."

"That's lame and you know it," Alex replied. She took another step down. "Am I going down alone?"

I forced my rubbery legs to move. "No. Wait up. I'm coming," I said.

I lowered my foot to the first stair. "But we'll only stay down for a second — right?"

"Just long enough to see if there is a Blob Monster hiding down there," Alex replied.

Waiting for fresh meat, I added silently.

I stumbled on the next step. But caught myself on the railing.

The candle flame dipped low, but didn't blow out.

The basement spread in front of us like a black pit.

We both stopped at the bottom of the steps — and listened.

Silence.

I raised the candle high. Tall stacks of cartons came into view. Behind them, I could see the two wooden wardrobe closets where Mom and Dad store our winter clothes.

"The Blob Monster could be hiding behind those tall cartons," Alex whispered. "Or in those closets."

I swallowed hard. "Alex — give me a break," I whispered back.

We made our way slowly to the stacks of cartons. I raised the candle high. We peeked behind the first stack.

Nothing hiding there.

"Can we go now?" I pleaded.

Alex rolled her eyes. "Don't you want to know the truth? Don't you want to know if your typewriter really has powers or not?"

"No. Not really," I whispered.

She ignored me. She grabbed the candle from my hand and moved behind the next stack of cartons.

"Hey — give that back!" I cried.

"You're too slow," she snapped. "Keep close behind me. You'll be okay."

"I'm not okay," I insisted. "I want to go back upstairs."

Alex moved quickly between the stacks of cartons. I had to hurry to keep up.

I never liked the basement. In fact, I was afraid of the basement even in the daytime.

I knew there really wasn't anything to be afraid of. But sometimes, telling yourself that doesn't do any good at all.

"Alex —" I whispered. "Can we —?"

I stopped when I heard the sound. A soft slapping, from somewhere against the wall.

Slap . . . slap . . . slap . . . slap . . .

Steady as a heartbeat.

Alex had moved away from me. I saw her walking quickly toward the laundry room.

"Alex —!" I hurtled across the room to her — so fast, I bumped into her.

"Hey — watch it!" she exclaimed.

"Alex — it's down here!" I shrieked. "It's here! It's really here! Listen! Do you hear it?"

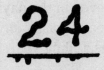

24

We both froze.

The steady, rhythmic sound rose up from the far wall.

Slap . . . slap . . . slap . . . slap . . .

"Do you hear it?" I whispered.

Alex nodded. Her mouth had dropped open in shock. She gripped the candlestick in both hands.

Slap . . . slap . . .

"What are we going to do?" I whispered.

"It's waiting for fresh meat," Alex murmured.

"I know. I know!" I groaned. "You don't have to say it." I pulled her arm. "Come on. We have to tell Dad."

I gazed through the darkness to the stairway. The steps seemed a million miles away.

"We'll never make it," I choked out. "We have to run past the Blob Monster to reach the stairs."

Slap . . . slap . . .

"What's our choice?" Alex shot back. "Pick one,

Zackie. Choice one: We stay here. Choice two: We don't stay here."

She was right, of course. We had to make a run for it.

Maybe if we ran fast enough, we'd take it by surprise.

Maybe the Blob Monster was too big to run fast.

Slap ... slap ... slap ... slap ...

"Let's go," Alex urged. "I'll go first since I have the light."

"Uh ... can we run side by side?" I asked softly.

She nodded.

Without another word, we took off.

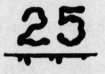

25

Our shoes thudded over the concrete basement floor.

I struggled to keep at Alex's side. My legs felt so heavy, as if I were running uphill!

"Whoooa!" I cried out when the lights flashed on.

Startled, we both stopped running.

I blinked hard, waiting for my eyes to adjust to the bright ceiling light.

Slap ... slap ...

We both turned to the far wall to see the Blob Monster.

And stared at a pale white hand slapping against the wall beneath the open basement window.

A *hand*?

Slap ... slap ...

"It — it's a rubber glove!" Alex exclaimed.

"It's one of Dad's gardening gloves," I choked out.

Dad usually leaves his heavy gardening gloves on that window ledge. One of the gloves was hanging from a nail. And the wind kept slapping it against the wall.

Alex laughed first. Then I joined in.

It felt good to laugh. And it felt especially good to know that no Blob Monster was hiding in the basement.

What a relief!

Alex and I climbed happily up the stairs. Then she made her way to the front door. "Thanks for the awesome entertainment!" she teased. "It was better than a movie! See you tomorrow."

She started out the door, then turned back. "We definitely got a little crazy tonight, Zackie. I mean, about that old typewriter."

"Yeah. I guess," I admitted. "It doesn't have any special powers. It didn't make a Blob Monster appear in the basement. And all the lights came back on without me having to type that they came on."

"The typewriter didn't cause *anything* to happen tonight. It was all coincidence," Alex said.

"Oooh. Big word!" I teased.

She slammed the door behind her.

"Are you doing anything, Zackie?" Mom asked.

"Not really."

It was Saturday afternoon, and I was just hanging out. I had a ton of homework to do. So I was lying on the couch, staring up at the ceiling, thinking up excuses not to do it.

"Can you run to the store for me?" Mom asked. "The Enderbys are coming for dinner, and I need a few things." She held up a slip of paper. "It's a short list."

"No problem," I said, climbing up from the couch.

Maybe I can add a few items to the list, I thought, taking it from her hand. Like maybe a few candy bars. Or a box of Pop-Tarts. . . .

I love to eat Pop-Tarts raw.

"Ride your bike, okay?" Mom asked. "I'm kind of in a hurry. Come straight back — okay?"

"No problem," I repeated. I tucked the list into the back pocket of my jeans and headed to the garage to get my bike.

The afternoon sun poured down. The air felt hot and dry. More like summer than spring.

I jumped onto my bike and pedaled down the driveway standing up. I turned toward town and sat down, pedaling fast, riding no-hands.

A few minutes later, I leaned my bike against the brick wall of Jack's. Jack's is mainly a meat market, but they sell fruits, and vegetables, and other groceries too.

The bell over the glass door clanged as I stepped inside. Mrs. Jack was at her usual spot, leaning her elbows on the counter beside the cash register.

Mrs. Jack is a big, platinum-haired woman with about a dozen chins. She wears bright red lipstick and long, dangling earrings.

She is really nice to everyone — except kids.

She hates kids. I guess she thinks we only come into her store to steal. When a kid comes in, she follows him up and down the aisles and never takes her eyes off him.

I closed the door behind me and reached into my back pocket for my shopping list.

Mrs. Jack had the newspaper spread out in front of her on the counter. She raised her eyes slowly and made a disgusted face at me. "Help you?" she muttered.

I waved the list. "Just buying a few things for my mom."

She grabbed the list out of my hand and squinted at it. Then she handed it back with a grunt. "Tuna is in the back on the bottom," she said.

"Thanks." I picked up a shopping basket and hurried to the back of the store.

A big air conditioner rattled against the wall. A fan in front of it blew cold air down the narrow aisle.

I found the tuna quickly and dropped two cans into my basket.

The long, white display counter of the meat department stretched in front of me. Behind the glass, cuts of red meat were lined up in perfect rows.

Beside the counter, an enormous side of beef hung from the ceiling.

That is really gross! I thought.

It looked like an entire cow — stripped of its hide — hanging upside down.

Yuck.

I started to turn away from it — when the dead cow moved.

It swung to the right, then swung back.

I stared in surprise.

The cow swung further, to the right, then back.

I watched it swinging on its rope, swinging heavily from side to side.

And then I heard a harsh, whispered voice:

"Fresh meat . . . Fresh meat . . ."

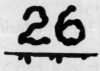

26

"Ohhh." A low moan escaped my throat as I gaped at the side of beef, swinging so slowly, back and forth, back and forth.

"*Fresh meat . . .*" came the raspy whisper again. "*Fresh meat . . .*"

"No —!" I blurted out.

I dropped my shopping basket.

And started to step back.

I let out another cry as Adam stood up and stepped out from behind the meat counter. He had a gleeful grin on his face.

"Fresh meat . . ." he whispered. And burst out laughing.

Annie and Emmy climbed out from behind the counter, giggling and shaking their heads.

"Awesome!" Annie exclaimed.

"Zackie, you're bright red!" her sister laughed.

My face burned as hot as the sun. I felt so embarrassed. How could I fall for such a dumb joke?

Now, I knew, they would tell everyone in school that I freaked out over a side of beef!

"What are you *doing* here?" I shrieked.

"We saw you on your bike," Adam replied. "We followed you into the store. Didn't you see us? We were right behind you."

"*AAAAGH!*" I let out a furious cry and balled my hands into fists.

"What's going on back there?" Mrs. Jack's harsh voice rattled the shelves. "What are you kids doing?"

"Nothing!" I called. "I — I found the tuna!"

I turned back to Adam and the twins. "Give me a break," I muttered.

For some reason, that struck them funny. They giggled and slapped one another high fives.

Then Adam stuck out both arms. He held them stiffly in front of him, like a sleepwalker. And began marching stiff-legged across the aisle toward me.

"You're controlling me, Zackie!" he declared in a machinelike voice. "I'm in your power."

He staggered toward me like some kind of zombie. "Your typewriter controls me, Zackie. Your typewriter has the power! I am your slave!"

"Adam — you're not funny!" I cried.

The girls giggled. They closed their eyes, stuck out their arms, and started marching toward me too.

"We're in your power," Emmy chanted.

90

"You're controlling our every move," Annie said.

"This isn't funny!" I shouted furiously. "Get lost, you guys! You —"

I turned and saw Mrs. Jack bouncing toward us, her face as red as her lipstick. "What are you doing back here?" she bellowed. "This isn't a clubhouse!"

Adam and the girls instantly lowered their sleepwalker arms. Annie and Emmy backed up against the meat counter.

"Are you buying anything?" Mrs. Jack demanded, huffing and puffing from her long journey from the cash register. "If you're not buying anything, get out. Go to the playground."

"We're going," Adam murmured. He couldn't get past Mrs. Jack. She filled the aisle. So he scooted down the next aisle.

Annie and Emmy hurried after him.

Mrs. Jack glared at me.

"I — I'm almost finished," I stammered. I picked up the basket. I searched for my list, but couldn't find it.

No problem. I remembered what was on it.

I found the other items and dropped them into the basket. Mrs. Jack stayed with me the whole while.

Then she walked me to the front of the store.

I paid and hurried out. I was so angry at Adam and the girls, I forgot all about the candy bars.

They are always making fun of me, I griped to myself.

Always playing mean tricks. Always trying to make me look like a jerk.

Always. Always.

And I'm sick of it. I'm sick to death of it!

"Sick sick sick!" I chanted the word all the way home. I hopped off my bike and let it crash to the driveway. Then I ran inside and tossed the grocery bag onto the kitchen counter.

"Sick sick sick."

I'm going to totally lose it if I don't cool down, I decided.

I ran up to my room and shoved a fresh sheet of paper into the old typewriter.

Then I plopped into the desk chair and furiously started typing. A third Blob Monster story. The scariest one of all.

I typed as fast as I could. I didn't think about it. I let my anger do the thinking.

I didn't write it out first. I didn't plan it. I didn't know what was going to happen next.

I leaned over the old typewriter and typed.

In the story, the ugly pink Blob Monster attacks the whole town. People are screaming. Running in every direction. Running for their lives.

Two police officers step forward to fight the Blob Monster off. It opens its huge mouth — and swallows them whole!

Shrieks of terror fill the town. The enormous Blob Monster is eating everyone alive!

"Yes!" I cried out loud. "Yes!"

I was paying everyone back. Paying the whole town back.

"Yes!"

It was the most exciting, most terrifying story I ever wrote. I wrote page after page.

"Zackie — you forgot something!" a voice called.

I started to type those words into the story. Then I recognized Mom's voice.

Breathing hard, I spun away from the type-writer. I found Mom leaning in the doorway, shaking her head fretfully.

"You have to go back to the store," she said. "You forgot the loaf of Italian bread. We need bread for dinner tonight."

"Oh. Sorry," I replied.

I glanced back at my story and sighed. It was going so well. I was having such a good time.

I'll get right back to it after I go to the store, I decided.

I took more money from Mom. Then I picked up my bike from the driveway.

I thought about my Blob Monster story as I pedaled to town. It's the best story I ever wrote, I decided.

I can't wait to read it to Alex.

I heard the thud of footsteps on the sidewalk. A

man in a business suit came running by. A dark blur. He ran so fast, I couldn't see his face.

What's *his* problem? I wondered. He's too dressed up to be jogging!

"Whoa!" I had to swerve to the curb as a blue station wagon roared toward me. The woman at the wheel honked her horn and waved frantically to me. Her tires squealed as she shot around the corner.

"Everyone is in such a hurry today," I muttered to myself.

Then I heard a scream. A man's scream.

I pedaled faster. I was a block from town. I could see the awning over the doorway of Jack's grocery on the corner.

I saw two people running past the store. Running at top speed, waving their hands.

I screeched to a halt when I heard another scream.

"Look out!" someone shrieked.

"Run! Call the police!"

Two little kids ran past me. One of them was sobbing.

"Hey — what's going on?" I called to them.

But they kept running. They didn't answer.

I started pedaling again, standing up. I leaned over my handlebars, trying to see what all the fuss was about.

As I reached town, I saw people running down

the center of the street. Cars honked. People were screaming.

"Hey — what's going on?" I called. "Is there a fire or something? Hey — somebody tell me what's happening. Somebody —"

And then I *saw* what was happening.

And I opened my mouth in a shrill scream of horror — and fell off my bike.

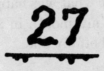

27

"OW!"

I landed hard on my right side. The bike slammed on top of me. The handlebar jabbed me in the neck.

A man ran past. "Get away, kid!" he shouted. "Hurry! Get away!"

I shoved the bike off me and climbed to my feet.

My heart pounding in my chest, I brushed myself off.

And gaped at the enormous, pink Blob Monster throbbing on the next corner.

"Ohhh." A horrified moan escaped my throat.

It looks just as I described it in my story! I realized.

Like a huge, slimy human heart. Pink and wet. With tiny black eyes. And purple veins knotted on top of its head. And a mouth cut into its belly.

Throbbing. Throbbing . . .

"It — it's *my* monster!" I cried.

Two little girls frowned at me as their mother

tugged them away. I recognized her. Mrs. Willow, who lives across the street.

"Zackie — run!" she cried, pulling each girl by a hand. "It's a horrible monster!"

"I know," I murmured.

She pulled her daughters across the street. But I didn't follow them.

I took a deep breath and made my way slowly down the street toward the throbbing Blob Monster.

I wrote this, I realized.

Just before I came to town, I typed this scene. I wrote that the Blob Monster attacked the town.

And I'll bet I know what happens next.

As I stepped closer, I saw the trail of thick slime the monster left behind it. Its belly pulled open, and I saw its purple tongue darting from side to side.

My legs trembled as I stepped even closer.

People screamed and ran. Cars and vans roared past, horns honking.

Everyone was running, desperate to escape. But I couldn't leave. I couldn't take my eyes off it.

I made you! I thought. Horrified and curious and amazed — all at the same time.

I created you!

I wrote this story!

The Blob Monster stared back at me through its tiny, black eyes.

Did it know who I was? Did it know that I created it?

As I stared in amazement, its mouth opened wider. It made sick, sucking sounds, and the purple tongue scraped the sides of its mouth.

Thick, yellow drool poured out of the open mouth. And the Blob Monster bounced forward.

Its purple tongue leaped out at me.

"Hey —!" I cried out. I struggled to back away.

The hot, sticky tongue wrapped around my leg. Started to pull me toward the slimy, open mouth.

"Let go!" I tugged on the tongue as hard as I could. "Help me!"

Two dark-uniformed police officers leaped in front of me. They had their nightsticks raised.

With angry cries, they both began pounding the throbbing creature.

POUND. POUND. POUND.

The nightsticks made a soft plopping sound with each hit.

The Blob Monster uttered a sickening gurgle. And its tongue slid off my leg.

"Run!" one of the officers screamed. "Get going!"

My legs were shaking so hard, I nearly fell. I could still feel the slimy, hot tongue on my leg.

I stumbled back.

And gaped in horror as the Blob Monster pulled open its mouth. The fat purple tongue swung around both police officers.

They beat it with their sticks. They shoved it. They tried to wrestle free.

But the tongue tightened, tightened around

them — and pulled them. Pulled them into the huge, open mouth in the creature's belly.

Pulled them both inside.

And then the mouth slammed shut with a disgusting *SPLAT*.

"No! Noooooo!" I wailed.

I wanted to pound my fists against the monster. Pound it until it melted to the ground.

"It's all my fault!" I screamed.

I wrote that scene with the policemen.

It was all in the story I had just typed. I wrote that the Blob Monster ate them both.

And now it had come true!

My frightening story had come true. Every scene of it.

The Blob Monster uttered disgusting gulping sounds as it digested its human meal. Its tiny black eyes locked on mine as it gulped.

What happens next?

What happens next in my story? I asked myself.

Trembling all over, my heart pounding, I struggled to think.

What happens next?

And then — with a shudder — I remembered what I had written.

The Blob Monster follows me home!

28

The Blob Monster made a final *gulp*. Then it opened its mouth in a disgusting, gassy burp.

Sickened by the sour odor, I staggered back.

I've got to think of something, I told myself. I've got to stop this monster.

Or it will eat me next.

The Blob Monster began to slide forward, plopping wetly on the sidewalk as it moved.

I knew I couldn't stand there another second. I spun away and forced my rubbery legs to run.

I picked up my bike off the street and jumped on. I began pedaling before I had my balance — and nearly crashed into a brick wall.

I struggled frantically to turn myself around, to calm down enough to ride. Finally, I pedaled away, groaning with each thrust of my foot.

I sped out of town. Halfway down the next block, I glanced back.

Yes. Just as I had written. The Blob Monster was following me. Bouncing rapidly over the pavement. The purple veins on top of its head bouncing with it. Behind it, a trail of slime thickened on the street.

It's so fast! I realized. It's keeping up with me!

What happens next? What did I type next?

"Oh, no!" I shrieked when I remembered.

This is the part where I fall off my bike!

"AIIIII!" My front tire hit a rock — and I went flying over the handlebars.

Once again, I hit the pavement hard. Once again, I shoved my bike off me and jumped to my feet.

I turned to see the Blob Monster catching up. Plopping quickly up the street, its mouth gaping open, its tongue stretching . . . reaching out for me.

I spun away — and ran into Alex and Adam.

"Run! Don't just stand there!" I screeched. "It — it's catching up!"

"Zackie — are you okay?" Alex asked.

"No time for questions!" I gasped, shoving them both. "Run! The Blob Monster is real! I wrote it — and now it's doing everything I wrote!"

Adam laughed. He turned to the Blob Monster. "Do you think I'm stupid, Zackie? This is a joke — right? What is that? Some kind of a balloon?"

"Adam — don't!" I cried.

I grabbed for him. And missed.

He went running up to the Blob Monster.

"Yeah. It's some kind of big balloon!" Adam repeated, grinning.

101

The monster's purple tongue slid quickly around Adam's waist.

It pulled Adam easily into the open mouth. And then the Blob Monster swallowed him with a sickening *gulp*.

Alex and I both screamed.

Alex turned to me. "Did you write that?" she demanded in a trembling voice.

I nodded. "Yes. It's in my story," I confessed.

Alex grabbed my shoulder. "Well, what happens next? Tell me. What comes next?"

"I — I don't know," I stammered. "That's where I stopped writing!"

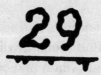

29

Alex and I never ran so fast in our lives. By the time we reached my house, my head was throbbing and my side was aching.

We both gasped for breath as I pushed open the front door. "Anyone home?" I shouted into the house. "Mom? Mom?"

No reply. She must have gone out.

I turned and glimpsed the Blob Monster bouncing hard over Alex's front yard.

"No time!" I cried to Alex. "No time! Hurry!"

She slipped inside the house, and I slammed the door behind us and locked it. Then I lurched toward my room, holding my aching side, forcing my rubbery legs to move.

I mopped the sweat off my forehead with my arm. Then I dropped into the desk chair and raised my hands over the typewriter keys.

Alex hurried up beside me. "What are you going to do?" she asked breathlessly.

"No time to explain," I choked out.

I heard a thumping at the front door. Then I heard a loud *CRAAAACK.*

And I knew the huge pink Blob had broken down the door.

"No time. No time!" I declared. I furiously started to type.

"I'm typing an ending," I told Alex. "I'm going to type that the Blob Monster disappears. That it never existed. That Adam and the two policemen are okay."

SQUISSSSH . . . SQUISSSSH.

Alex and I both gasped. We heard the Blob Monster's slimy body, so close now, moving quickly toward us through the hall.

I knew I had only a few seconds to type the ending.

SQUISSSSSSH.

Right outside my bedroom door.

I held my breath and pounded the keys.

Pounded as hard and fast as I could until —

"NOOOOO!"

"What's wrong?" Alex shrieked.

"The keys are jammed!"

We both screamed again as the Blob Monster bounced into the room.

30

The Blob Monster's body heaved up and down. The creature panted, its entire body bouncing. White slime puddled on the floor around it.

The slash of a mouth in the belly opened and closed, opened and closed. The purple tongue licked the mouth as the monster's eyes narrowed on me.

Alex gasped and backed up against the wall. "Zackie — type the ending!" she screamed breathlessly. "Make that thing disappear!"

"I *can't!*" I cried. I frantically pulled at the keys. "They're jammed. I can't untangle them!"

"Zackie — *please!*" Alex pleaded.

And then I saw the fat purple tongue leap.

It rolled out of the Blob Monster's open belly like a garden hose.

"NOOOOOO!" I opened my mouth in a terrified wail as the tongue stretched across the room. Reached for me . . .

Reached for me . . .

No!

The tongue wrapped around the typewriter. Lifted it easily.

I grabbed for it with both hands.

And missed.

My hands slid across the tongue. So hot. Burning hot. And sticky.

The tongue pulled back, snapped back like elastic. And carried the typewriter into the monster's gaping mouth.

As I stared in horror, the Blob Monster swallowed the typewriter with a single *gulp*.

I leaped up from the desk chair. And stepped up beside Alex. We pressed our backs against the wall and watched helplessly as the Blob Monster throbbed and heaved. Digesting the typewriter.

"We're doomed," Alex murmured. "The typewriter — it's gone. Now there is no way you can destroy the monster."

"Wait!" I cried. "I have an idea!"

31

I dove back to the desk. I searched the desktop.

"What are you *doing*?" Alex cried.

The Blob Monster let out sick gurgling sounds as it digested the typewriter. Its body heaved up and down in the puddle of slime it had left on the rug.

"The pen," I told Alex. "The pen —"

I pulled open the desk drawer and saw the old pen in front. I grabbed it and slammed the drawer shut.

I held it up to show Alex. "The old pen the woman gave me. Maybe it has the same powers as the typewriter. Maybe I can write an ending with the pen — and make the Blob Monster disappear!"

"Hurry —!" Alex warned.

The Blob Monster had stopped its gurgling. The purple tongue came darting out again.

I grabbed a sheet of paper and leaned over the desk. I pulled off the cap on the pen and lowered the point to the paper.

"THE —"

I wrote one word — and felt something hot and wet slap against the side of my face.

The fat purple tongue slid against me.

"Ow!" I cried out. And dropped the pen.

My hand shot up to my cheek, and I felt hot, sticky slime.

My stomach heaved.

The tongue curled around the old pen. And carried it to the Blob Monster's mouth.

"Noooo!" Alex and I shrieked together.

The creature sucked the pen into its open belly, and began its digesting gurgles.

"Now what?" Alex asked in a whisper. "What can we do? It's going to eat *us* next!"

I jumped to my feet. The desk chair toppled over.

I stepped away from it, my eyes on the doorway. "Make a run for it!" I cried.

Alex held back. "We can't," she sighed. "That thing — it's blocking the way. We'll never get past it."

She was right. The Blob Monster would stick out its tongue and pull us easily into its drooling mouth.

"Try the window!" I cried desperately.

We both turned to the window.

No way. It was bolted shut because of the air conditioner.

"Doomed," Alex whispered. "Doomed."

We both turned back to the throbbing, pink monster.

And then I had one more idea.

"Alex — remember when Adam typed something on my story? And it didn't come true?"

She nodded, keeping her eyes on the gurgling Blob Monster. "Yes, I remember. But so what?"

"Well," I continued, "maybe that's because it's *me* that has the power. Maybe the power isn't in the typewriter or the pen. Maybe I got the power that night in that antique shop when I was zapped by that electrical shock."

Alex swallowed hard. "Maybe . . ."

"Maybe it's been in *me* the whole time!" I cried excitedly. "All I have to do is *think* what I want to happen — and it will come true. I don't have to type it or write it. I just have to *think* it!"

"Maybe . . ." Alex repeated.

She started to say something else. But the Blob suddenly bounced forward, squishing over the rug. And its tongue rolled out toward us.

"Ohhhh . . ." Alex backed up against the wall.

The fat tongue licked her arm. It left a thick smear of sticky drool on her skin.

"Think fast, Zackie!" Alex cried.

The tongue curled and started to wrap itself around Alex.

"Make it disappear!" Alex pleaded. "Think! Think it away!"

109

I froze in horror as the fat tongue wrapped around Alex. It lifted her off the floor.

Screaming, she thrashed her arms and kicked. Squirming frantically, she wrapped her hands around the sticky tongue — and shoved with all her strength.

But the disgusting tongue squeezed tighter, held her in its slimy grip.

I shut my eyes.

Think! I instructed myself. Think *hard*!

Think that the Blob Monster is gone.

Gone . . . gone . . . gone.

I held my breath. And thought with all my might.

Would it work?

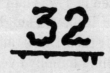

The monster is gone.

That's what I thought.

The monster is gone . . . gone . . . gone . . .

I silently chanted the word, over and over. Then I opened my eyes.

And the Blob Monster was gone!

Alex stood in the center of the floor, a dazed expression on her face. "It . . . it worked," she choked out.

I *do* have the power! I realized.

I closed my eyes again and started to think. *Adam is back,* I thought.

Adam is back . . .

I opened my eyes — and Adam stood beside Alex.

He blinked several times, then squinted at me. "What's happening?" he asked.

"I have it!" I cried happily. "I have the power — not the typewriter!"

"What are you *talking* about?" Adam demanded. "What power?"

I shook my head. "You wouldn't understand," I told him.

Alex started to laugh.

Before I realized it, I was laughing too.

Joyful laughter. Relieved laughter.

All three of us stood there, laughing, laughing, laughing — laughing happily ever after.

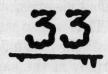

33

"Well? Did you like my story?"

The pink Blob Monster neatened the pages he had just read and set them down on the desk. He turned to his friend, a green-skinned Blob Monster.

"Did you just write that?" the green monster asked.

The pink Blob Monster gurgled with pride. "Yes. Did you enjoy it?"

"I did," his friend replied. "Thank you for reading it to me. It's very exciting. Very well written. What do you call it?"

"I call it 'Attack of the Humans,'" the Blob Monster replied. "Did you really like it?"

"Yes. Those humans are really gross," his friend replied. "Do you know my favorite part?"

"What part?"

"When the Blob Monster ate Adam. That was really fun!" the green creature declared. "But I have just one problem with your story."

The pink Blob Monster bobbed up and down. The veins on top of his head turned a darker purple. "A problem with my story? What is it?"

"Well..." his green friend replied. "Why did you give it such an unhappy ending? I hated it when the human shut his eyes, and the Blob Monster disappeared. That was so sad."

"Do you think so?" the pink monster asked, gazing down thoughtfully at the pages he had written.

"Yes," his friend replied. "You should have a happy ending, instead. Everyone likes a happy ending."

The pink Blob Monster picked up his story. "Okay. You're right. I'll change the ending. I'll have the Blob Monster eat them all!"

"Great! I love it!" his friend declared. "Now, *that's* a great ending!"

ADD MORE

GOOSEbumps®

TO YOUR COLLECTION...

HERE'S A CHILLING PREVIEW OF
THE NEW COLLECTOR'S EDITION OF

NIGHT OF THE
LIVING DUMMY

"Mmmmm! Mmmm! Mmmmm!"

Kris Powell struggled to get her twin sister's attention.

Lindy Powell glanced up from the book she was reading to see what the problem was. Instead of her sister's pretty face, Lindy saw a round pink bubble nearly the size of Kris's head.

"Nice one," Lindy said without much enthusiasm. With a sudden move, she poked the bubble and popped it.

"Hey!" Kris cried as the pink bubble gum exploded onto her cheeks and chin.

Lindy laughed. "Gotcha."

Kris angrily grabbed Lindy's paperback and slammed it shut. "Whoops — lost your place!" she exclaimed. She knew her sister hated to lose her place in a book.

Lindy grabbed the book back with a scowl. Kris struggled to pull the pink gum off her face.

"That was the biggest bubble I ever blew," she said angrily. The gum wasn't coming off her chin.

"I've blown much bigger than that," Lindy said with a superior sneer.

"I don't *believe* you two," their mother muttered, making her way into their bedroom and dropping a neatly folded pile of laundry at the foot of Kris's bed. "You even compete over bubble gum?"

"We're not competing," Lindy muttered. She tossed back her blond ponytail and returned her eyes to her book.

Both girls had straight blond hair. But Lindy kept hers long, usually tying it behind her head or on one side in a ponytail. And Kris had hers cut very short.

It was a way for people to tell the twins apart, for they were nearly identical in every other way. Both had broad foreheads and round blue eyes. Both had dimples in their cheeks when they smiled. Both blushed easily, large pink circles forming on their pale cheeks.

Both thought their noses were a little too wide. Both wished they were a little taller. Lindy's best friend, Alice, was nearly three inches taller, even though she hadn't turned twelve yet.

"Did I get it all off?" Kris asked, rubbing her chin, which was red and sticky.

"Not all," Lindy told her, glancing up. "There's some in your hair."

"Oh, great," Kris muttered. She grabbed at her hair but couldn't find any bubble gum.

"Gotcha again," Lindy said, laughing. "You're too easy!"

Kris uttered an angry growl. "Why are you always so mean to me?"

"Me? Mean?" Lindy looked up in wide-eyed innocence. "I'm an angel. Ask anyone."

Exasperated, Kris turned back to her mother, who was stuffing socks into a dresser drawer. "Mom, when am I going to get my own room?"

"On the Twelfth of Never," Mrs. Powell replied, grinning.

Kris groaned. "That's what you always say."

Her mother shrugged. "You know we don't have a spare inch, Kris." She turned to the bedroom window. Bright sunlight streamed through the filmy curtains. "It's a beautiful day. What are you two doing inside?"

"Mom, we're not little girls," Lindy said, rolling her eyes. "We're twelve. We're too old to go out and play."

"Did I get it all?" Kris asked again, still scraping pink patches of bubble gum off her chin.

"Leave it. It improves your complexion," Lindy told her.

"I wish you girls would be nicer to each other," Mrs. Powell said with a sigh.

They suddenly heard shrill barking coming from downstairs. "What's Barky excited about now?"

Mrs. Powell fretted. The little black terrier was always barking about something. "Why not take Barky for a walk?"

"Don't feel like it," Lindy muttered, nose in her book.

"What about those beautiful new bikes you got for your birthday?" Mrs. Powell said, hands on hips. "Those bikes you just couldn't live without. You know, the ones that have been sitting in the garage since you got them."

"Okay, okay. You don't have to be sarcastic, Mom," Lindy said, closing her book. She stood up, stretched, and tossed the book onto her bed.

"You want to?" Kris asked Lindy.

"Want to what?"

"Go for a bike ride. We could ride to the playground, see if anyone's hanging out at school."

"You just want to see if Robby is there," Lindy said, making a face.

"So?" Kris said, blushing.

"Go on. Get some fresh air," Mrs. Powell urged. "I'll see you later. I'm off to the supermarket."

Kris peered into the dresser mirror. She had gotten most of the gum off. She brushed her short hair back with both hands. "Come on. Let's go out," she said. "Last one out is a rotten egg." She darted to the doorway, beating her sister by half a step.

As they burst out the back door, with Barky yipping shrilly behind them, the afternoon sun was high in a cloudless sky. The air was still and dry. It felt more like summer than spring.

Both girls were wearing shorts and sleeveless T-shirts. Lindy bent to pull open the garage door, then stopped. The house next door caught her eye.

"Look — they've got the walls up," she told Kris, pointing across their backyard.

"That new house is going up so quickly. It's amazing," Kris said, following her sister's gaze.

The builders had knocked down the old house during the winter. The new concrete foundation had been put down in March. Lindy and Kris had walked around on it when no workers were there, trying to figure out where the different rooms would go.

And now the walls had been built. The construction suddenly looked like a real house, rising up in the midst of tall stacks of lumber, a big mound of red-brown dirt, a pile of concrete blocks, and an assortment of power saws, tools, and machinery.

"No one's working today," Lindy said.

They took a few steps toward the new house. "Who do you think will move in?" Kris wondered. "Maybe some great-looking guy our age. Maybe great-looking twin guys!"

"Yuck!" Lindy made a disgusted face. "Twin guys? How drippy can you get! I can't believe you and I are in the same family."

Kris was used to Lindy's sarcasm. Both girls liked being twins and hated being twins at the same time. Because they shared nearly everything — their looks, their clothing, their room — they were closer than most sisters ever get.

But because they were so much alike, they also managed to drive each other crazy a lot of the time.

"No one's around. Let's check out the new house," Lindy said.

Kris followed her across the yard. A squirrel, halfway up the wide trunk of a maple tree, watched them warily.

They made their way through an opening in the low shrubs that divided the two yards. Then, walking past the stacks of lumber and the tall mound of dirt, they climbed the concrete stoop.

A sheet of heavy plastic had been nailed over the opening where the front door would go. Kris pulled one end of the plastic up, and they slipped into the house.

It was dark and cool inside and had a fresh wood smell. The plaster walls were up but hadn't been painted.

"Careful," Lindy warned. "Nails." She pointed to the large nails scattered over the floor. "If you step on one, you'll get lockjaw and die."

"You wish," Kris said.

"I don't want you to die," Lindy replied. "Just get lockjaw." She snickered.

"Ha-ha," Kris said sarcastically. "This must be the living room," she said, making her way carefully across the front room to the fireplace against the back wall.

"A cathedral ceiling," Lindy said, staring up at the dark, exposed wooden beams above their heads. "Neat."

"This is bigger than our living room," Kris remarked, peering out the large picture window to the street.

"It smells great," Lindy said, taking a deep breath. "All the sawdust. It smells so piney."

They made their way through the hall and explored the kitchen. "Are those wires on?" Kris asked, pointing to a cluster of black electrical wires suspended from the ceiling beams.

"Why don't you touch one and find out?" Lindy suggested.

"You first," Kris shot back.

"The kitchen isn't very big," Lindy said, bending down to stare into the holes where the kitchen cabinets would go.

She stood up and was about to suggest they check out the upstairs when she heard a sound. "Huh?" Her eyes widened in surprise. "Is someone in here?"

Kris froze in the middle of the kitchen.

They both listened.

Silence.

Then they heard soft, rapid footsteps. Close by. Inside the house.

"Let's go!" Lindy whispered.

Kris was already ducking under the plastic, heading out the doorway opening. She leaped off the back stoop and started running toward their backyard.

Lindy stopped at the bottom of the stoop and turned back to the new house. "Hey — look!" she called.

A squirrel came flying out a side window. It landed on the dirt with all four feet moving and scrambled toward the maple tree in the Powells' yard.

Lindy laughed. "Just a dumb squirrel."

Kris stopped near the low shrubs. "You sure?" She hesitated, watching the windows of the new house. "That was a pretty loud squirrel."

When she turned back from the house, she was surprised to find that Lindy had disappeared.

"Hey — where'd you go?"

"Over here," Lindy called. "I see something!"

It took Kris a while to locate her sister. Lindy was half hidden behind a large black Dumpster at the far end of the yard.

Kris shielded her eyes with one hand to see better. Lindy was bent over the side of the Dumpster. She appeared to be rummaging through some trash.

"What's in there?" Kris called.

Lindy was tossing things around and didn't seem to hear her.

"What *is* it?" Kris called, taking a few reluctant steps toward the Dumpster.

Lindy didn't reply.

Then, slowly, she pulled something out. She started to hold it up. Its arms and legs dangled down limply. Kris could see a head with brown hair.

A head? Arms and legs?

"Oh, no!" Kris cried aloud, raising her hands to her face in horror.

A child?

Kris uttered a silent gasp, staring in horror as Lindy lifted him out of the Dumpster.

She could see his face, frozen in a wide-eyed stare. His brown hair stood stiffly on top of his head. He seemed to be wearing some sort of gray suit.

His arms and legs dangled lifelessly.

"Lindy!" Kris called, her throat tight with fear. "Is it — is he . . . *alive*?"

Her heart pounding, Kris started to run to her sister. Lindy was cradling the poor thing in her arms.

"Is he alive?" Kris repeated breathlessly.

She stopped short when her sister started to laugh.

"No. Not alive!" Lindy called gleefully.

And then Kris realized that it wasn't a child after all. "A dummy!" she shrieked.

Lindy held it up. "A ventriloquist's dummy," she said. "Someone threw him out. Do you believe it? He's in perfect shape."

It took Lindy a while to notice that Kris was breathing hard, her face bright red. "Kris, what's your problem? Oh, wow. Did you think he was a real kid?" Lindy laughed scornfully.

"No. Of course not," Kris insisted.

Lindy held the dummy up and examined his back, looking for the string to pull to make his mouth move. "I *am* a real kid!" Lindy made him say. She was speaking in a high-pitched voice through gritted teeth, trying not to move her lips.

"Dumb," Kris said, rolling her eyes.

"I am *not* dumb. You're dumb!" Lindy made the dummy say in a high, squeaky voice. When she pulled the string in his back, the wooden lips moved up and down, clicking as they moved. She moved her hand up his back and found the control to make his painted eyes shift from side to side.

"He's probably filled with bugs," Kris said, making a disgusted face. "Throw him back, Lindy."

"No way," Lindy insisted, rubbing her hand tenderly over the dummy's wooden hair. "I'm keeping him."

"She's keeping me," she made the dummy say.

Kris stared suspiciously at the dummy. His brown hair was painted on his head. His blue eyes moved only from side to side and couldn't blink.

He had bright red painted lips, curved up into an eerie smile. The lower lip had a chip on one side so that it didn't quite match the upper lip.

The dummy wore a gray double-breasted suit over a white shirt collar. The collar wasn't attached to a shirt. Instead, the dummy's wooden chest was painted white. Big brown leather shoes were attached to the ends of his thin, dangling legs.

"My name is Slappy," Lindy made the dummy say, moving his grinning mouth up and down.

"Dumb," Kris repeated, shaking her head. "Why Slappy?"

"Come over here and I'll slap you!" Lindy made him say, trying not to move her lips.

Kris groaned. "Are we going to ride our bikes to the playground or not, Lindy?"

"Afraid poor Robby misses you?" Lindy made Slappy ask.

"Put that ugly thing down," Kris replied impatiently.

"I'm not ugly," Slappy said in Lindy's squeaky voice, sliding his eyes from side to side. "You're ugly!"

"Your lips are moving," Kris told Lindy. "You're a lousy ventriloquist."

"I'll get better," Lindy insisted.

"You mean you're really keeping it?" Kris cried.

"I like Slappy. He's cute," Lindy said, cuddling the dummy against the front of her T-shirt.

"I'm cute," she made him say. "And you're ugly."

"Shut up," Kris snapped to the dummy.

"You shut up!" Slappy replied in Lindy's tight, high-pitched voice.

"What do you want to keep him for?" Kris asked, following her sister toward the street.

"I've always liked puppets," Lindy recalled. "Remember those marionettes I used to have? I played with them for hours at a time. I made up long plays with them."

"I always played with the marionettes, too," Kris remembered.

"You got the strings all tangled up," Lindy said, frowning. "You weren't any good at it."

"But what are you going to *do* with this dummy?" Kris demanded.

"I don't know. Maybe I'll work up an act," Lindy said thoughtfully, shifting Slappy to her other arm. "I'll bet I could earn some money with him. You know. Appear at kids' birthday parties. Put on shows."

"Happy birthday!" she made Slappy declare. "Hand over some money!"

Kris didn't laugh.

The two girls walked along the street in front of their house. Lindy cradled Slappy in her arms, one hand up his back.

"I think he's creepy," Kris said, kicking a large pebble across the street. "You should put him back in the Dumpster."

"No way," Lindy insisted.

"No way," she made Slappy say, shaking his head, his glassy blue eyes moving from side to side. "I"ll put *you* in the Dumpster!"

"Slappy sure is mean," Kris remarked, frowning at Lindy.

Lindy laughed. "Don't look at me," she teased. "Complain to Slappy."

Kris scowled.

"You're jealous," Lindy said. "Because I found him and you didn't."

Kris started to protest, but they both heard voices. Kris looked up to see the two Marshall kids from down the block running toward them. They were cute redheaded kids that Lindy and Kris sometimes babysat for.

"What's that?" Amy Marshall asked, pointing at Slappy.

"Does he talk?" her younger brother, Ben, asked, staying several feet away, an uncertain expression on his freckled face.

"Hi, I'm Slappy!" Lindy made the dummy call out. She cradled Slappy in one arm, making him sit up straight, his arms dangling at his sides.

"Where'd you get him?" Amy asked.

"Do his eyes move?" Ben asked, still hanging back.

"Do *your* eyes move?" Slappy asked Ben.

Both Marshall kids laughed. Ben forgot his reluctance. He stepped up and grabbed Slappy's hand.

"Ouch! Not so hard!" Slappy cried.

Ben dropped the hand with a gasp. Then he and Amy collapsed in gleeful laughter.

"Hahahaha!" Lindy made Slappy laugh, tilting his head back and opening his mouth wide.

The two kids thought that was a riot. They laughed even harder.

Pleased by the response she was getting, Lindy glanced at her sister. Kris was sitting on the curb, cradling her head in her hands, a dejected look on her face.

She's jealous, Lindy realized. *Kris sees that the kids really like Slappy and that I'm getting all the attention. And she's totally jealous.*

I'm definitely *keeping Slappy!* Lindy told herself, secretly pleased at her little triumph.

She stared into the dummy's bright blue painted eyes. To her surprise, the dummy seemed to be staring back at her, a twinkle of sunlight in his eyes, his grin wide and knowing.

Copyright © 1993 by Scholastic Inc.

About the Author

R.L. Stine's books are read all over the world. So far, his books have sold more than 300 million copies, making him one of the most popular children's authors in history. Besides Goosebumps, R.L. Stine has written the teen series Fear Street, the funny series Rotten School, as well as the Mostly Ghostly series, The Nightmare Room series, and the two-book thriller *Dangerous Girls*. R.L. Stine lives in New York with his wife, Jane, and Minnie, his King Charles spaniel. You can learn more about him at www.RLStine.com.

THE SCARIEST PLACE ON EARTH!

EnterHorrorLand.com

SCHOLASTIC and associated logos are trademarks and/or registered trademarks of Scholastic Inc.

■ SCHOLASTIC

GBHLB

The Original Bone-Chilling Series

Now with All-New Behind-the-Screams
Author Interviews and More!

SCHOLASTIC and associated logos are trademarks
or registered trademarks of Scholastic Inc.

FOXDVD

© 2007 Protocol GB Productions 3 Inc. In Trust All Rights Reserved. SCHOLASTIC, G, GOOSEBUMPS and associated logos are trademarks and/or registered trademarks of Scholastic Inc. All rights reserved. © 2007 Twentieth Century Fox Home Entertainment LLC. All Rights Reserved. TWENTIETH CENTURY FOX, FOX and associated logos are trademarks of Twentieth Century Fox Film Corporation and its related entities.